Influence of the Moon

Influence of the Moon

Mary Borsky

The Porcupine's Quill

I want to thank Al Campbell, Frances Itani, Sheelagh Teitelbaum, the Ottawa Writers' Group, and most especially John Metcalf. I am also grateful for the generous assistance of the Banff Centre for the Arts, the Canada Council Explorations Programme, the Ontario Arts Council, and the Regional Municipality of Ottawa-Carelton.

These stories are imagined and are not intended to represent real people or events.

Table of Contents

For Tatiana Nadkrynechny

Ice

WHEN THE RUSSIANS shot a dog up into space, my father celebrated for three days. Later, when he got sober, he took us fishing, me and my brother Amel.

'B.B. Hunt and the other guys, when it's Russian, they think it's something bad,' my dad said. He almost had to shout to be heard above the pounding of the tire chains on the winter road. Amel and I sat next to him on the front seat of the dark blue Dodge. I was wearing boys' clothes, the same as Amel, a parka, extra pants, tuque, winter boots.

'But you and me, we like that dog in space, don't we Daddy?' I shouted back. 'We think it's fine, right Daddy?' Amel and I were drinking root beers. It pleased me to sit with a bottle in my hand and talk of grown-up matters to my dad.

'The Russians,' my father said, shifting down to go up a hill, 'when they want to send a dog in space, do they ask The-Important-B.B.-Hunt, or do they just go ahead and do it?'

I took a moment to drain the last of my root beer. Sometimes I didn't understand anything my father said – Power of the Proletariat, Science and Progress, the Emancipation of the Working Man. Still, I believed every word he said.

'They just go ahead, Daddy,' I said. 'They don't ask anybody.' Then I checked my father's face, although I was pretty sure I'd answered right.

As we neared the crest of the hill, I could at last see the lake through the grey tops of trees. The ice, mostly blown clear of snow, was grey and flat as a cookie pan, so bright in a strip where the sun reflected, it was impossible to look at. The sky was as blue as the spark from an electric plug.

'Look,' I said, pointing to the bay in the distance. 'The fishing shacks.'

My father watched the road ahead.

Then, to show whose side I was on, I added, 'They look like outhouses on the ice.'

'Some guys,' my father said, 'they got to have a shack to keep the wind off. They got to have a chair to sit on. They got to have a piece of paper to tell them what to catch.'

He and Amel laughed out loud, and I tried to join in.

I'd heard about those new fishing shacks at school. I'd heard they weren't shacks at all, but almost a home away from home. Gwen Farris put up her hand for News and told us that inside there was a real stove, a little table to sit beside, a window to watch the road, even a calendar on the wall.

I put my hand up too.

'Teacher,' I said, pleased to contribute, 'my dad doesn't do the same as every other Joe Blow. My dad catches more fish than anybody. My dad fishes with nets and catches as much as he feels like.'

'Now, Irene Lychenko,' the teacher said gravely, 'is this *News?*' She paused while I tried to remember. 'Remember, boys and girls, News is something you didn't already tell us the day before.'

Beside me on the front seat of the car, I felt Amel turning and looking.

'Daddy!' he yelled. 'It's The-Important-B.B.-Hunt!'

I turned to see a two-tone yellow Buick starting to pull up beside us.

Without moving his head, our dad looked into his side mirror, then stepped harder on the gas. The tire chains hammered faster on the snowy road, then slowly our car pulled ahead again.

'Here's the turn!' Amel called out, and Daddy made a sudden lurching left to the lake, exploded through a small snowdrift, then drove quickly down the trail to the fishing shacks.

I didn't like the look of B.B. Hunt following close behind in the blowing snow. He had a dark, definite look, the look someone following you home from school might have. But it was all right now, because we were with our dad, and it was fun, being first.

As we approached the shacks, I studied them quickly, taking in what I could. I saw brown walls, orange window frames, possibly the flash of green curtains. Our dad aimed the car between the shacks and shot through, chains hammering, right onto the lake.

The car fishtailed, once, then twice.

'Wheeee!' Daddy said, each time he straightened the wheel. 'Wheeee!'

We laughed, then a minute later, laughed again.

Suddenly there was a loud bang, like a gun going off, then smaller cracking noises. I felt the ice shift under us. I sat up straight and grabbed the door handle on my right, and Amel's arm on my left.

'Scared?' our dad laughed.

Amel looked at me and laughed too.

'Why be scared?' our dad said. 'You got to use your head! You got to think! We're the same as flies walking across a piece of newspaper!' He took his hands off the steering wheel and criss-crossed his fingers to illustrate. 'The Russians,' he said, 'they're scared of nothing!' And he continued to drive straight out onto the lake as if we were in a high, fast boat.

'That dog, Daddy,' I said, 'is it a real dog?'

'Real! What you talking about? You betcha it's real!' He pointed his finger through the windshield up toward the bright blue sky. 'First, they send up a dog, and next! ... A man!'

Suddenly, he braked, turned off the ignition, got out and unloaded the trunk.

Outside, in the stinging cold, I looked up where my father had pointed. There was nothing, only a blueness so intense I had to grab onto the car because it felt, for a moment, as though I would fall up into it.

Amel and I watched as our father started to chop a hole in

the ice, but it took too long. We began to slide in our boots and to swing each other with a rope from the car.

The ice was hard and clear, with tiny bubbles frozen into it, like the glass of marbles. Here and there the ice was buckled, as if the waves themselves had frozen. In other places, the ice was black and clouded over with white, as frightening to look into as Old Man Coons' bad eye.

When our father finished chopping the hole, the ice was as thick as the length of his arm, the water a black hole.

We watched as he dropped in his net, let it straighten in the current, spiked it to the ice, then walked off fifty yards to chop another hole.

From time to time, there was a rumble, like the sound of distant thunder.

'Listen,' our dad yelled from where he was. 'The ice!'

Sometimes the rumble branched away before it reached us. Other times, it passed through the area where we were. I stood very still and listened.

Finally, when the cracking stopped, and I was sure I could hear nothing but the breathing of the wind on the ice, I grabbed Amel's hands and we spun in a circle.

'To Peace! To Progress!' Amel yelled, raising his imaginary glass to me. 'To ... to ... porridge!'

I clinked back. 'To pancakes!' I screamed, though not as well, because my teeth ached from laughing in the cold and I had to keep my lips pulled over them.

Then our dad pulled his nets out, and loaded the flopping fish into the trunk of the car.

'Fifty-seven!' he grinned, holding a pickerel up to show us.

But Amel and I were cold and went to wait in the car.

The sun had set, leaving a crayon-line of gold along the horizon. The ice was now blue-purple, the sky, violet. The first stars were out. Amel started to cry with cold.

Finally our dad opened the door. His eyebrows were bushy with frost.

'The satellite!' he said. 'Come and look-it!'

Amel wouldn't look. He was crying and kicking under the dash.

'You want to see that dog?' our father asked me. 'Come and see that dog!'

I was cold, but I got out. Daddy stood behind me, positioning my head and pointing to something high up.

'There!' he said. 'See it?' His hand was dark, and very large against the sky.

I looked. There was only sky, stars, and cold.

'Over my finger! It looks like a star, but it's moving!'

Then I saw it.

It was a regular yellow star, not the dog-shape I'd expected. And the star was moving, very slowly and evenly sideways. I squinted my eyes to see better. It didn't look like anything I'd ever seen before. It looked like a trick. It looked as if the star was being pulled sideways by a long invisible string.

'Where's the *dog*?' I asked, stamping my half-frozen feet. I was almost in tears. My face felt like wood. There were sharp shooting pains in my fingers.

'The dog's inside!' my dad said. 'It's in a steel ball! Look! It's so high the sun is shining on it!' He sounded as if he was shivering.

I looked once more at the moving point of light.

'What *colour* of dog?' I demanded.

'Any colour! Colour's all the same!'

I hurried back to the car at the same moment that Amel started to pound on the horn.

Daddy got in behind the wheel, started the motor, switched the heat fan on full, and drove quickly back toward shore.

The car smelled of fish and cold exhaust.

My feet ached even more as they started to thaw out under the heater.

'You think it's *easy* to shoot a dog into space?' our dad asked as he drove. 'You think it's something simple?'

I cried to myself and drained the pop bottles for stray drops. Amel whimpered, rocking back and forth over his folded arms.

Out of the dark, the fishing shacks loomed up. Outside the shacks, there were two cars now, The-Important-B.B.-Hunt's, and another one. The other car had its headlights on and someone was loading the trunk. Several of the men were standing shoulder to shoulder, arms crossed, beside one of the shacks. Someone's cigarette glowed red in the dark.

Our father drove between the shacks and braked. Our car swung a little to the side. Daddy unrolled his partly frosted window, and put his elbow out. He took off his cap, then put it back on.

'Nice night, boys!' he called through the swirling exhaust. 'Seen the sky tonight, boys?'

I stopped crying to pay attention to what was happening.

Someone said his name.

'Get a look at that north sky, boys?' our dad asked, grinning.

'Fishing trip, Lychenko?' someone from the line-up said. It was B.B. Hunt.

'Why, sure,' Daddy said. 'You bet.'

'Catch many?' B.B. Hunt asked, still from where he stood.

'One or two. Seen the sky tonight, B.B.?'

'One or two! You gotta be joking!' B.B. yelled. He came up to our window, bringing the smell of whisky and shaving lotion with him. He put his hands on the window ledge.

I looked at The-Important-B.B.-Hunt's Volunteer Fire Brigade crest on one side of his parka, the fuzzy Curling Championship crest on the other. On his pale puffy hand I saw a gold ring with a square dark stone.

'One or two!' B.B. hollered again, looking back to check that his friends were listening. 'Cripes, Lychenko, you're a pitiful excuse for a fisherman! You're a washout! We done better than that over here!'

None of us moved. Then I heard an odd wavery voice that

took me a split second to recognize as my own.

'My dad got fifty-seven!'

B.B. Hunt's teeth were as even as if they'd been lined up against a ruler. They shone white even in the dark.

'Nice,' B.B. said. 'That's nice. A guy tends to get a good catch with a square hook, don't he? Open the trunk and let's have us a look-see, Lychenko.'

'Ha-ha,' my dad said. 'Careful, B.B. ... You gonna make me laugh.'

'This son-of-a-bitch Communist is through disregardin' the laws of the land!' B.B. hollered. 'This is a citizen's arrest and I got witnesses!'

He jerked the car door open, then our dad was on the ice and B.B. Hunt was on top of him.

Everything was happening too fast.

'Break it up, boys, break it up,' one of the other men said.

Then The-Important-B.B.-Hunt was on his back on the ice, his mouth gasping like a pickerel's, a strip of white belly showing, and our dad was getting up, wiping his mouth, looking at his hand. He got into the car, started the stalled motor, and pulled away.

There was a commotion outside, yelling, then pounding on the trunk of the car. My dad rolled up his window and speeded up. Something hard, a bottle or a piece of ice, hit the top of the car, and Daddy speeded up again.

The car moved quickly down the side road, heaved itself up onto the highway, turned right, then sped down the road to town.

'She's not supposed to tell, is she, Daddy?' Amel said, crying. 'How come she told?'

Our dad drove fast, sometimes checking in the rearview mirror.

Then without warning, he skidded to a stop in his tracks. He got out, went to the trunk, and made several trips to the side of the road. I heard branches snap as he threw things into the bush. Then the trunk slammed and he was back, breathing hard, but behind the wheel.

'Will Daddy go to jail?' Amel cried, pulling at my arm. 'I don't want Daddy to go to jail.'

The sound of the chains pounding against the road roared in my ears. I held myself very still, as if to slow down what was happening.

We cut through the darkness in an almost straight line. I could see no light anywhere, except for our own yellow head-lights, no familiar house or fence or sign.

There was the rapid hammering of chains, but the motor of the car itself seemed silent. Our dad was behind the wheel, but it seemed to me that he was not really driving. We were being pulled by some other thing. We were being pulled by the same trickery that had pulled the dog in its steel ball.

I turned to my father to warn him. I wanted to tell him what had happened. Or maybe to tell him I believed the things he said. 'Daddy,' I wanted to say, 'I saw it, the dog, the star, the steel ball.'

But in that half-moment before I spoke, I sensed some shift or lurch, some darkness in the air between us.

My father looked different as he hunched low behind the wheel. His face looked rumpled. His cap was gone, and I remembered now seeing the cap lying on the ice. Without it, and in the dark, he looked like someone else. He looked different than my dad.

I didn't say anything. Neither did he. From my place at the window I watched and waited. White trees appeared from the blackness, flew past, and disappeared again.

Above, there were stars everywhere, in front of us and behind, but there were too many and we were moving too fast to see any one separate from another.

The Bible Seller

THE BLACK MAN at the door showed me the white book in his hand.

'The Holy Bible,' he said, and put a cardboard suitcase down at his feet. 'I have others, but this particular is a favourite with young ladies such as yourself.'

He unzipped the book, holding it out for me to see, then fanned the pages. The edges of the pages were gold, and something – the book or the black man – smelled very nice, of jam maybe, or cinnamon candy.

The man was wearing a pale blue suit, a white shirt, and a tomato-red tie, the same slant of red as the red of my mother's wedding dress.

'Pictures,' the man announced, 'rendered by the artist in full-colour.'

From the corner of my eye I noticed the movement of something white – a blouse or a scarf – behind the hedge.

It was the Widow-Lady, who'd moved in next door and smiled with lipsticked lips at my dad, calling out in her sandpapery voice, 'Nice night! Pure heaven, except for the flies!'

I turned my shoulder against the Widow-Lady, stepped closer to the black man and bent down to see his book. I saw people doing things, wearing clothes the colours of Kleenex flowers.

'Moses parts the Red Sea,' the black man said, holding the pictures out for me to see. 'The soldier offers drink to Christ on the cross. Is your mama home?' His mouth was as red as if a flashlight was shining into it.

'No,' I said. I could feel the Widow-Lady's eyes on the back of my neck.

A bug buzzed suddenly from the bush beyond the Widow-

Lady's house, and the man swished something away from his ear.

'Is she at the store, honey?'

'No,' I said, and cleared my throat, sorting out in my head what things to say about my mother. I had to keep two piles separate, the good, and the not-so-good.

'Never mind that, honey,' the black man said, twisting his neck to give himself more room in his collar. 'Just bring me the man of the house.'

I opened the screen door and stepped in, letting the door slam on its spring behind me. 'Just a minute,' I said, and went through the dark, echoey front room and out the back door of the kitchen.

I ran barefoot down the back alley, refusing to look up from the road until after I'd passed the Widow-Lady's house. I pounded my heels hard against the ground to shake off the feeling of her eyes following me, the sight of her nylons drying on the fence, the picture in my head of the way she opened her mouth a few seconds before she spoke, a fish after a fly.

It took two or three minutes to get through the patch of bush, past the bus depot, and to the poolroom where my dad worked.

* * *

'My mum is gone,' I'd told the Widow-Lady, who'd asked. The caragana hedge was tall and scraggly with open spaces in the middle where the lady could watch.

'Gone?' the Widow-Lady said, holding her wrinkled throat with her hand. 'Oh, your pore dad. Your pore, pore dad. And who is cooking for him, pray tell?'

Her hair was bobby-pinned into pin-curls in the front, pink-foam curlers in the back, and wrapped around with a white see-through scarf.

I cooked, but didn't feel like telling her. I cooked ordinary toast and French toast, raisin and plain, all colours of Jell-O, Kraft dinner, canned beans, and fried baloney.

I picked a yellow flower from the caragana and sucked it. It had the smallest bit of sweetness, like a single grain of sugar.

'Where did she go *to*, your mama?' the Widow-Lady asked again, pushing her curlered head through the bushes to hear.

'To the city,' I said, pleased with the brisk sound of it. 'She went to the city.'

* * *

Everything was black when my mother woke me. There was no light at all, except a yellow strip that came under the door from the kitchen.

'I'm taking the bus,' she said. She was sitting on the edge of my bed, tipping me against her. 'I can't get rid of this broken-glass feeling inside my head. I don't know what's happening to me. They're sending me to the hospital in the city.'

It seemed to me I was dreaming, or maybe sick with fever. I closed my eyes and saw the broken glass she was talking about. I started to dream I was gathering it into a Pyrex mixing bowl.

Then I woke again when I heard her voice beside me.

'If anything happens to me, go to school.'

I felt her press something small and flat into my hand.

'Here's the bank book,' she said. 'Your family allowances are in the bank. If I don't come back, keep going to school. Don't show it to your dad. Just go to school.'

In the darkness, I could smell mothballs, which meant she was going somewhere, to the store for groceries, or to the doctor about the feeling in her head.

In the morning, the thin blue bank book was in my bed. I got up to check the faded red couch in the front room where my mother slept now, but she wasn't there.

Every morning when I woke, I checked the couch to see if she'd come home on the bus during the night, but every morning, the couch was empty.

'Mama,' my dad said, glancing out the window as if someone might be listening from the road, 'Mama, she's crazy in the head. The doctors can't do nothing for her.'

He showed me how to use the wringer washer, smiling as he fed clothes through the rubber rollers, to show how easy it was. He showed me how to scrub around the burners of the stove, instead of letting the crumbs burn off. He bought some scouring pads in a box that said Chore Girl.

I thought of how my mother told me things she read in the *True Story* magazines she kept behind the wood box.

'Somewhere I read,' she said, 'about a woman who married a truck driver, only he was really a movie star. Somewhere I heard about someone who fell in love with the stunt-rider at the rodeo.'

We were picking raspberries beside the highway.

'Don't get married,' she said. 'Not till you're twenty-three or twenty-four. Don't get married young like I did.'

I swished my hair to keep the bugs from my face.

'What dress did you wear to get married, Mama?'

'Just an everyday dress.'

She kept her eyes on the berries as she spoke, so as not to lose her place. She dropped the wine-red berries silently into her nearly full pail.

'You have more than enough time to get married,' she said.

'I know,' I answered, waiting for her to fill her pail so she could pick into mine. 'Is that dress for everyday, Mama? The one you have on?'

My mother was wearing a cotton house dress, tomato-red with buttons that had outlines of white sailboats.

'I don't know,' she said. 'I guess so.'

I thought of my mother marrying my dad and wearing that dress, the tomato-red dress with the sailboat buttons.

Later, I tried to remember whether my mother kissed me before she left. What I remembered was the smell of mothballs, the broken glass gathered into a Pyrex mixing bowl, the cold thin feel of the bank book, and how in the morning the red couch was wide and empty, with no one on it.

* * *

Inside the poolroom where my dad worked, I tried to duck in behind the counter before the men saw me. But they saw me anyway, pushed back their caps and cowboy hats, laughed, wolf-whistled, and pounded the ends of their pool-cues on the floor.

'Boss! Hey, boss! You got a lady lookin' for you!'

As my eyes got used to the smoky dimness, I could read the signs my mother'd made with purple crayon on the backs of corn flakes boxes. NO PROFANITY, the signs read, every few feet along the wall, NO PROFANITY.

Then, from the blue smoke, my dad appeared.

I cupped my hands to his ear to tell him about the black man, about his pale blue suit, about his tomato-red tie, about the palms of his hands which were the colour of newborn mice. I told about the white book, about the pictures, about the money that would be required for such a book.

'What?' my dad said, looking at me and leaning down to hear. 'You come for that?'

He opened the door of the poolroom, threw down an empty Coke crate to prop open the door, then turned back to grin at the men.

'Nuts,' he laughed. 'Everybody's goin' nuts!'

He put his hand into his deep jangly pocket and brought out keys for the chocolate bar case.

'Have a bar!' he said, 'any bar! It's on the house!'

I took a chocolate bar and went outside with it. Everything around, the brown grain elevators, the bus depot, the telephone poles, looked very bright and sharp-edged, as if they'd been cut out of paper.

Back at the house, the black man wasn't on the front steps where I'd left him. He wasn't beside the pin-cherries at the side, and there was no one in the tall grass at the back. The door of the toilet hung open on its hinges exactly as it always did, the pages of the catalogue ruffling a little with sun and flies.

I went into the back door of the house.

Right away, I could tell the Widow-Lady had been there. There was a hint of perfume, the smell of something good to eat.

On the middle of the blue-painted kitchen table was a pie left by the Widow-Lady. The pie was golden-brown, crimped prettily along the edge, and sprinkled with sugar.

I would drop the pie down the well, I told myself, and say ha ha for you. I would hide it in the cellar. I would feed it to Old Man Coons' three-legged dog named Nipper.

But instead, I cut myself a piece of pie and took it onto the back steps.

The pie was peach. It was good but not that good.

'Make a pie,' my dad said to me once, thinking of it when he was sanding a T-shaped section for a wooden ball he was making. He invented things, a wind-powered propeller boat, a knife that snapped out of a wooden comb, a secret compartment for whisky in a nail keg. The ball he was sanding was really a puzzle. It came apart, but no one except himself could put it back together.

'Why don't you make a pie.'

'I don't know how to make a pie,' I said.

'Look,' he said, finding a recipe in the paper. 'Just do what they say. Flour, lard, apples, sugar.' I looked at the long stretch of grey print in the paper and the grainy grey picture of the pie half-way down.

I didn't believe it. I didn't believe you could make a pie just like that. When my father went back to his ball, I put the news-paper in the wood box along with the kindling.

I finished the Widow-Lady's peach pie and left my dirty plate on the back steps. I stuck my hands into the rainbarrel and scrubbed them dry on my skirt.

It was hot in the weedy grass, but purple clouds were

starting to roll in on one side of the sky. From far away, I heard the wagon-on-the-road sound of thunder.

The black man wasn't anywhere. There was no one on the road. There was no one in the Widow-Lady's yard either, although I could hear her laugh, then laugh again from inside her house.

Maybe I'd made the black man up, I thought. Maybe I'd fallen asleep and dreamed him.

Through the windows and screen door, our house looked dark, and much too quiet. What if I went in and found something awful. What if I went in and my mother in her red wedding dress was dead on the couch.

The high purple clouds moved in, but the sun still slanted yellow underneath. Everything, the trees, our house, the caragana hedge, shone with an intense gold light.

I felt prickles on the skin of my arms and legs, and my mouth tasted like batteries. It was very still.

Then something like a train flew through the air. There was a crash that shook the earth, the air, the sky.

I was on the ground.

My dad was there.

'Did you see?' he said, his eyes lit up like he was inventing something. 'Did you see? Lightning went through the house.'

He went up to the front door and I followed him.

'Look,' he said, pointing. 'It melted through the screen.'

He opened the front door and I followed him into the dark house.

I turned my head to look. There was no one on the couch.

'Look at the table,' my dad said, going into the kitchen. The blue paint on the table was burnt off in a snaking black line, and nothing remained of the pie but a handful of lumpy black cinders.

'Look where it went out,' he said, pointing with a trembling hand to the doorframe that was charred black along the inside edge.

We stood and stared at the melted screen, the scarred table, the cinders, the blackened doorframe.

The air was the colour of plums. I felt hollow and clear inside, like a whistle cut from willow. It seemed to me I was almost weightless in the purple air.

When I turned to my dad, at first I couldn't see him at all. Then, to the left of me, I saw the white of his face and his hands.

We stood side by side at the burnt-out doorframe. On the roof I heard what seemed like mice. Then on my face and neck and arms, I felt a fine hard mist of rain.

The Blue Dress

AUNTIE ROSE, who wrote in green ink every week but who'd been away for my whole life, was asleep on our front room couch. Outside her screened window, I hummed to myself, stuck sticks into ant tunnels, sang songs into the rainbarrel.

'Blue lake and rocky shore, I will return once more,' I sang. The rainbarrel vibrated in my hands. Maybe I should be a radio singer, I thought. 'Boom-diddie-Boom-boom ...'

A hand clamped down on my arm and steered me sharply to the side of the house.

'Ssshhh!' My mother's face pressed down close to mine. 'Ssshhh! She's sleeping! Let her sleep!'

I waited for her to loosen her grip on my arm. 'If you can't behave out here,' she said, 'then come in. Come in and set the table.'

I followed her in, running my hands over the heads of the pom-pom dahlias that were staked along the side of the house.

During the night, I'd heard Auntie Rose come in with my mother who'd gone to meet her at the bus depot. I heard their voices, quick and quiet through most of the night, usually Auntie Rose's, sometimes my mother's, sometimes both of them together. Once, I got out of bed and saw white suitcases, yellow hair, the flash of red fingernails, then lay down again, listening to the tangle of their voices, smelling the coffee, the perfume, the cigarettes.

I'd waited so long to see her, I thought as I followed my mother in through the back screen door, but I still had to wait some more. What if I snapped in two like a marshmallow stick? What if I burst into flame like the marshmallow itself?

The kitchen seemed as dark and cool as the rainbarrel. From

my parents' bedroom off the kitchen I could hear my dad snoring, like a drawer opening and shutting. I wondered if I could lay out the forks and spoons before my eyes got used to the dark, turned quickly to the drawer, and bumped into a chair.

'Don't wake your dad either,' my mother said. We stopped moving to listen, but he was still snoring. 'You're not a baby anymore, Irene,' my mother said. 'You're big now. I shouldn't have to watch you like a hawk.'

She was dressed in her best clothes, a newly ironed white blouse, a brown print skirt, and shoes she hardly ever wore because they made her baby toes curl under. Her hair was freshly curled and pinned straight back with a row of bobby-pins.

'Give her the plate with the roses,' my mother said, standing straighter than usual and frowning to hide her smile.

I placed the honey jar on the table, and at that moment, a ray of sunshine entered the room, struck the jar, and scattered. All four walls were dappled in wavy light.

My eye caught on high-heeled shoes outside the front room door. They were as red and shiny as if they'd been dipped in nail polish. One was upright, the other on its side.

'Look,' I said to my mother, squatting down to see them. My mother bent down too.

'Don't get your fingerprints on them,' my mother said, then stood and went back to the stove, where she folded her arms and hunched her shoulders. 'Rose was always the brave one,' she said. 'Something different or something new, Rose wasn't scared to do it.'

My mother turned back to the stove, and I could hear the hiss of the propane for a moment before it exploded gently into a flower of blue flame. The smell of propane hung in the air.

'Me, I was the other way around,' my mother said. 'I was scared of my own shadow. Whatever they told me, I did it. When they said, ''Marry'', I did it. If they said, ''Don't marry'', then I wouldn't have.' She turned the blue flame low and put the frying pan over it. 'If someone said, ''Jump in the lake'', I guess I'd do that too.'

* * *

Auntie Rose was the one who was supposed to marry my Dad. My mother told me the story many times, when she was darning my dad's socks, or when she was putting Auntie Rose's latest letter into the green ribbon where she kept all of Rose's letters.

'Rose was the oldest, so our parents – your Baba and Grampa – they said she should marry first. But Rose said, No, no, no, she'd rather die. She wouldn't eat. She wouldn't get out of bed.'

'She didn't want to marry Daddy?' I asked. I always stumbled on this. Why would anyone not want to marry my dad?

'He was old and we were young. The first time we saw him we laughed and said, ''Who's the old crow?'' Then, wham, out of the blue, suddenly Rose was supposed to marry him.'

'Did Daddy want to marry her?'

'For a man,' my mother said, 'it's different. A man needs a woman to cook for him and keep his clothes clean.' She was silent for a while, frowning at the sock she was darning on the heel of her hand. She wove the yarn evenly in and out, working in the ends so as not to leave any knots or lumps.

'Rose wouldn't talk,' my mother said. 'She wouldn't eat, not even strawberries. Then suddenly, one morning, she got up, washed her hair and braided it with ribbons on the top of her head. She said, ''I want to get my wedding dress in town, I want a modern-days wedding dress from the Red and White''.

'So your dad and my dad – they must have been scared she'd change her mind – right away they harnessed the horses and loaded the wagon with wheat to sell to buy the wedding dress. Then, once they got to town, Rose ran away.'

'Why didn't they stop her?'

'They sold the wheat – your dad and my dad – they told Rose to go ahead and buy the dress, then they went to the beer parlour to celebrate. And when they came out, Rose was gone.'

My mother finished one sock, pulled it tight to check the mending, then pulled another on her hand. 'Served them right,' she said. 'I wish I could've seen their faces.'

'She didn't buy the dress?' I asked.

'She never set foot in the Red and White. They said they never even saw her. She wasn't with the horses. She wasn't visiting her friend who married the elevatorman. Finally, when it was getting dark, your dad and my dad went to the RCMP. The RCMP said she must have left town on the bus. They said it happened once before. They said a girl shouldn't be set loose in town with the money for a wedding dress.'

This part of the story always stunned me. I could see the too-empty wagon, the horses, shaking their harnesses, sensing something was wrong, the sun, red on the horizon. I thought of the unbought dress, the fruitless search, my grandfather, my father, all of us forever deprived of the yellow-haired Rose.

'Why did she do it?' I asked.

'Look at her,' my mother said. 'She's made something out of herself. She's got a good job and fancy clothes. She goes bowling with her friends if she feels like it. For her, it was good.' She stabbed the needle back into the heart-shaped pin-cushion. 'For me, maybe it wasn't so good.'

My mother sighed and in one motion, balled up the pile of socks, impatient now that we'd reached the other part of the story, the part we were living out now, the part where she married Daddy, they moved to town and I was born.

'Who would I be if Daddy was the one who married Auntie Rose?' I asked. 'Would I still be me?'

'How would I know? You'd be the same I guess.'

I thought about myself with a mother who wore fancy clothes, ate pears out of cans, and went bowling with her friends when she felt like it.

'Would my name be *Irene?*'

'It didn't happen, so why think about it?'

* * *

From the front room, there was a loud yawn, a footstep. My mother straightened her shoulders and quickly smoothed down her skirt. The front room door opened, and Rose stood before us.

Her lips were a red bow, her hair yellow and curled down to her shoulders. She wore a long apricot-coloured dressing gown of shiny satin, matching high-heeled slippers, and in her red-tipped fingers she held a package of cigarettes and a gold lighter. She was so bright I could hardly look at her.

'Irene, Irene,' she said, carrying a little breeze of perfume to me. 'Don't be shy, honey.' She put a perfumy apricot arm around me and kissed me on the cheek. She was as soft and smooth as a flower petal.

'She wouldn't keep quiet,' my mother said.

'I thought I heard a birdie singing,' Rose said, and winked at me. I stood beside her chair, hardly able to breathe.

'I wanted you to sleep a while,' my mother said. 'I wanted Gilbert to go to work before you got up.'

'Wilma, don't worry about it. I'm not afraid of Gilbert. I deal with all kinds of people at work. Believe me, I've seen every type.' She took a cigarette from the package, placed it between her red lips, flicked the large gold lighter, then sucked the smoke in.

'My white coat is ruined, Wilma. That bus ride was so long and dusty. It seemed to go on forever. I thought I'd die. At the back, there were people drinking and yelling. Everyone else just sat there like ... like *livestock*, taking whatever was dished out to them.' Auntie Rose inhaled again, held it a moment, then smiling at me, blew the smoke high into the air.

'I couldn't live here, Irene,' she said. 'I just couldn't.'

I could hardly believe that she was speaking straight to me.

'They're not supposed to drink on the bus,' I offered, my voice just above a whisper. 'They're supposed to do what the driver says.'

'Just like you,' my mother snapped. 'Just like you do what someone says.' She poured the coffee into Auntie Rose's cup.

Auntie Rose put her apricot-satin arm around me again. 'Go to the front room, honey, and bring back the two white boxes from the table.'

I went into the darkened front room, transformed now into a garden of Auntie Rose's clothes, bottles, brushes, and mirrors. I touched a necklace of orange pearls, then brought back the boxes.

Auntie Rose took the larger one, and held it out to me. 'This one's for you, sugarlump.'

I opened the box and inside was a blue dress. It tumbled softly down in my hands. It was made of shimmery blue taffeta, with soft flounces around the neckline, and all down the skirt. I'd never seen anything so beautiful.

'Try it on,' Auntie Rose smiled. 'Put it right over your shirt and shorts.'

I put it on and it rustled softly down to my knees. Auntie Rose and my mother laughed.

'You look like a movie star,' my mother said, pleased.

'This one's for you, Wilma,' Rose said, giving the small flat box to my mother. My mother dried her hands hard, reached for the box, and from tissue paper, brought out a long scarf, striped in yellow and red. My mother looked at one side, the other, then read the label.

'It's a *scarf*, Wilma,' Rose said.

'It's pretty,' my mother said, and she folded it back into its tissue paper, into the box, and put the box up on the shelf beside the clock.

'Don't put it away, Wilma,' Rose said, 'wear it.' Then pinching her cigarette between her lips, she got the scarf from its box and wrapped it around my mother's neck. My mother stood still while Rose tucked it inside the neckline of her blouse, then frowning against the smoke, pulled it out, then tucked it in again.

Auntie Rose turned to me for an opinion.

'It's pretty,' I said. 'It's pretty, Mama.'

'You have to learn to wear scarves, Wilma,' Rose said, sitting down again. She looked up and down at my mother's clothes while my mother stood there. 'Maybe it's the brown skirt. No one under forty should wear brown, Wilma. Not unless you want to look forty.'

My mother turned without speaking, and spread bacon in the frying pan.

It was silent in the room except for the sizzle of bacon and the regular burp of the coffee pot. From my parents' bedroom I heard coughing. The sun shone directly into the room now and everything was bright. My dress shone as blue as the propane flame.

My mother turned to me. 'You better take off that dress,' she said. 'You're going to spill something on it.'

'Let her wear it, Wilma,' Rose said. 'Let her be pretty.' She smiled at me, lifted one of my hands and looked closely at it. 'I'll do you a manicure later, honey, just like I do for my customers at the store. We'll have you looking just like your Auntie Rose in no time flat.'

'Hello, Rose,' I heard my father say. He was standing in the darkened doorway of my parents' bedroom, holding his hand out to Auntie Rose. He was unshaven, but dressed in his dark baggy clothes, and his teeth were in.

My mother shut the bedroom door behind him.

'Look at my dress, Daddy,' I said. 'See my dress?'

'Hello, Gilbert,' Rose answered, reaching her hand out too, then settling it on her cigarettes.

My father jingled the money in his pockets.

'See my dress, Daddy?' I said, jumping up and down as if powered by a wind-up spring. 'See my dress?'

'So ...' Rose said, lighting a cigarette, cradling one elbow in the palm of her other hand and smiling. 'So, tell me, Gilbert, how's everything?'

'Good,' my dad grinned, showing the too-pink gums of his false teeth. 'Everything's going good.'

'My dress!' I shrieked, still jumping. 'My dress! My dress!'

'Stop it!' my mother said, and slapped my arm.

I stood rigid beside the table.

My father pulled out his chair and sat down. He turned to me. 'You got a dress?'

I turned and ran out the back screen door.

'It's look but don't touch with her,' I heard my mother say.

I walked rapidly up and down the sidewalk beside the house, the blue dress rustling. Words sparked in my mind. *Who says? So what? Think twice. Watch out.* I walked up and down again. *Damn.* I looked up and down the road. *If a bus comes by, I'll take it.*

I remembered the bus that Auntie Rose took, and thought of her getting on with her cigarettes – no, with her ribboned braids. She got on, then turned in the doorway to see me coming.

'Come on, honey,' she called. 'You've got to hurry. Hurry, Irene, before they see us.'

I ran to her in my flame-blue dress, the dress rushing against my legs. I stepped up to the first high step of the bus. The air smelled of dust and hot exhaust. Auntie Rose reached down for me, took my hand and pulled me up. 'I couldn't live here, Irene,' she said. 'I just couldn't.'

'Irene, Irene,' another voice called me. 'Irene, you gotta show me your dress.'

It was my dad, from inside the house. I looked in through the fly-pocked screen and saw him sitting across from my mother and apricot-robed Auntie Rose. They were talking and laughing.

Quickly, I turned away, and as I walked, twisted one of the

flounces on the skirt of my dress. I twisted it into a rope and pulled, but nothing happened. Then I pushed the fabric of the dress down onto one of the stakes from the pom-pom dahlias, pressed harder, until suddenly, the stick tore through the blue taffeta then roughly, down. I felt the shock of it in my bones. There was a deep scratch on my wrist too, and I watched a moment until a drop of blood welled to the surface.

I looked at the tear in my dress, then tried to smooth it with my hands. It wouldn't smooth though, not even when I spat on it and rubbed it harder. It gaped like a wound.

I didn't understand it, that it wouldn't get fixed. Why was it, that things wouldn't go backwards?

Queen of the Land

MY SISTER, BABY, was in the hospital and I held Elsie Potts to blame. Elsie'd poked sharpened pencils into Baby's arms and legs, playing Nurse, and left five tiny blue holes in Baby's skin.

'It's Elsie's fault,' I told my mother. 'Baby wouldn't be in the hospital if it wasn't for Elsie Potts.'

'Then stop hanging around those Pottses like you don't have a home to go to,' Mama said.

The smell of scorched cotton hung in the air. My mother'd just ironed my dad's shirts, and was sitting down now to crack sunflower seeds with her teeth and read about Princess Margaret in the *Star Weekly*.

'It says here that Royalty, they only wear their clothes one time. See this hat?' she asked, and pointed to a picture of Princess Margaret with a hat. 'She wears it once and that's it. Next time she just orders them to bring her a new one.'

I twirled a piece of my hair around my finger, twisting it into a rope, let it go, then twisted it again.

'A couple pokes with a pencil aren't going to hurt anybody,' Mama said. 'The doctor just wants to do some tests. Baby's run down is all. Maybe they'll put her on a tonic.'

Pokes with a pencil aren't going to hurt anybody? I asked myself. That's a awful interesting commentary.

Then I couldn't help but notice how fine those words sounded in my head.

'That's a awful interesting commentary,' I said into the grey afternoon air of the kitchen.

'Styles come and styles go,' Mama read aloud, running her finger along the lines as she read, 'but the Royal hemline never changes.'

She looked up at me in wonderment, sunflower seed shells

scattered down the front of her sweater.

I looked away, holding to myself this hard, sweet secret: I was the one that Baby loved best.

I was the one who knew to put Baby's milk and Rice Krispies in separate bowls. I cut her toast in diamonds, not in squares. Sometimes after school, I did her hair with a curling iron and took her to look at things in the Red and White.

People would stop and talk to her. 'Whoops! Got your nose!' they said, or 'Give Auntie that pretty pink dress! Boo-hoo-hoo! Auntie's crying for that pretty pink dress!'

Baby hid her face in my skirt, pulling on it, so I would know to bend down and let her whisper her answers in my ear. 'No,' I answered for her. 'No. No.'

Then sometimes, I flipped into reverse. Suddenly, it drove me crazy how she stuck to me like glue, how she copy-catted me, how she wouldn't stop talking. 'I spy with my little eye. I dreamt of peaches, did you dream of peaches? Watch me. Guess which. Look here.'

I plugged my ears and hummed when she talked. I told her I was really someone else and just wearing a mask. Other times, I ran off to play with Elsie Potts and left Baby crying at the gate.

* * *

Elsie sat at the front of my row in grade five, near the blackboard by her mother's request. Elsie was the tallest and heaviest girl in the class, the only one with a grown woman's body. She was two or three years older than the rest of us. Elsie had been born simple, my mother claimed, in punishment for things Elsie's mother, Mayva Potts, had done wrong.

'What things?' I asked, my breath seizing up for a moment. It always scared me when the topic of Mayva Potts's wrongdoings came up.

'Let's just say she was not exactly a angel.'

'Maybe she didn't know it was wrong. Maybe she didn't mean it.'

'Everyone knows the difference between right and wrong,' my mother said grimly, but with a faint smile.

Would I know? I asked myself. I didn't know if I'd know.

Most women in town wore housedresses during the day – loose cotton print dresses that were cheaper than regular ladies' dresses. My mother didn't. She wore party clothes her sister in the city sent her to wear out. And Mayva Potts didn't wear housedresses either. She wore good ladies' dresses which she ordered from the catalogue, and she dressed Elsie in the same type of dress – dresses most people saved for going to the doctor's or for Sundays – flowered rayons pleated at the waist, lilac crepes, gabardines with matching jackets.

Mayva Potts was always Mayva Potts, never Mrs Potts or even Miss Potts. They lived with Mayva Potts's father, Old Man Potts, in a tiny green house behind the post office.

Mayva and Elsie were a common sight on the streets of town, walking back and forth to the Hall of Christian Brethren, or on their various visitations to the old and the sick. Because of their fine clothes and their similar squarish shape, Elsie and her mother were impossible to tell apart from a distance, except by their walk. Both of them walked with the slow, steady pace I imagined sailing ships would have, but Mayva sailed along like a ship in good weather, while Elsie leaned forward a little at the waist, as if she was leaning into a storm.

Every flat surface of the Pottses' tiny kitchen and living-room was taken up with the different things Mayva was always making to give away to the old and sick when she paid her visits – paper plates with Bible verses spelled out in alphabet macaroni and spray-painted silver, artificial flowers made of old nylon stockings dyed different colours and stretched over loops of wire, crosses made of burnt matches glued to a board so it looked like the cross had been singed by fire.

Once Mayva brought a questionnaire to our door that she'd written out by hand on a sheet of lined scribbler paper. Each question had a box to tick off yes or no.

Have you experienced the Awesome Power of God's grace?
Do you wish for the Peace that Passeth all understanding?
Do you wish that your Personal Life was fuller and more
   abundant?
Do you long to be washed in the Blood of the Lamb?
There were eleven questions in all.

My mother read the questionnaire outside in the yard, then went in to work out her response at the kitchen table, using my school dictionary to get it exactly right. She wrote her reply across the bottom of the questionnaire in her small, tight handwriting, capital letters standing no higher than the lower-case.

Decent people don't go nosing around where they are not invited. CARDINAL RULE NUMBER ONE. *Kindly refrain to disturb me at the vicinity of my place of residence.*

Then she folded the questionnaire and gave it to Elsie to return to her mother.

'No man in the picture,' my mother explained, her eyes on an old shirt she was cutting into strips to add to the rag rug.

I still didn't see what she meant. There was a man. There was Elsie's grandpa, Old Man Potts, who couldn't stand noise in the house, the same as my dad.

* * *

Usually it was Elsie's idea to get Baby and take her to Elsie's house.

We feasted on Mayva's diet milkshakes and puddings, painted Baby's fingernails with nailpolish, sprayed her with cologne, clipped gold earrings on her ears, and pushed her in an old baby buggy.

'Make way for the queen of the land,' we called, as we pushed her around the block.

'That's the trouble with you,' my mother said when I brought Baby home, bedraggled and tired, 'you're not happy if you're not hounding someone.'

* * *

I grabbed Elsie on the way to school and pushed her into the dirty crust of snow that still remained in the bushes.

Served her right, I told myself, that her boots filled up with lumps of snow, that her mottled old-lady legs got scratched by branches.

This bush was my own territory anyway, being nearer my house than Elsie's. I could do what I wanted there, except when the Gooderhams, who travelled in a pack, took it over.

'It was you that did it, wasn't it?' I accused. 'It was you that poked her with a pencil. You're the one. You're the one that made her sick. Don't think you can get away with it.'

Elsie pulled her neck into her shoulders and pushed her glasses up. She was wearing a red wool coat with a Persian lamb collar. Pinned to the collar was a corsage Mayva'd made, a cluster of tiny tin bells with no tongues in their throats.

'Don't you dare try that again,' I said to Elsie who stood where I'd pushed her. 'Don't you ever dare.'

I walked away, but when I looked back, I was relieved to see her following me again. Still, in the shadows of the cloak-room, I reached up and shook her until her glasses slipped down.

* * *

The summer before, Elsie and Baby and I planted a garden in the bush. It was Elsie's idea, and she hung stubbornly on to it like a dog to its dinner.

How would we get a shovel? I argued. How would we get seeds? I knew there wasn't enough sun. How would we keep the Gooderhams from wrecking it?

But Elsie wouldn't let the idea go, won Baby to her side, and finally I was forced to take a fresh look at it.

We would plant peas, we decided, corn on the cob, strawberries, and a row of blue carnations, which Elsie had seen at a wedding at the Hall of Christian Brethren.

'Can't you stop pestering me?' Mama said, when we went to her for seeds. 'Nothing's going to grow in the bush. I'm not giving you seeds so you can throw them away for nothing.'

She was working in her own garden, hoeing the already weedless rows between the cabbages to make sure no weeds appeared. She was wearing a turquoise-coloured satin blouse with a fern pattern woven into it, and a flowered circle skirt with fancy pockets on the sides.

Elsie, Baby and I stood silently on a board by the rainbarrel, three crows on a fence, and watched.

Finally, Mama stood up and wiped her upper lip on the ruffled collar of her blouse.

'If you want, you can have a potato,' she said, and got one from the sack in the porch. 'You can cut it into pieces, but you have to leave one eye in every piece.'

'I know that already,' I said, taking the potato, but careful not to touch her hand.

We picked a spot in the bush off the main path, and hacked at it with a hoe. Baby was given the job of pulling grass. The ground was tough with roots and fibres and rocks. We could only soften the ground a few inches at the top, and in some places, not at all. Still, we cut the potato into four pieces and planted the pieces, each piece in its own spot.

We watered the potatoes with water we carried from the culvert. We did this several times that same day, then we forgot about it.

* * *

One day it was winter and the next day it was spring. Flies appeared between the storm-windows. The breeze was warm and fragrant with the smell of mud. When I came home from school at noon-hour to strip off my scratchy winter stockings, the phone rang. It was the hospital. Baby's tests were finished, and she could go home.

'I'll go,' I said to Mama, who'd just washed and shrunk the

front room curtains and now had to sew a border along the bottom. 'You don't need to go. I'll go.'

Mama got clean clothes for Baby, and my dad and I drove to the hospital.

The car smelled of mothballs, because our dad had just changed his long underwear for the lighter summer weight. It snagged in my mind that my mother might be angry, but I left my boots behind at home, and wore shoes.

'Nice day!' people called from the rolled-down windows of their cars.

'You bet!' my dad called back, and found some music on the radio.

'I know where to go,' I said when we got there, and my dad turned off the engine, but left the key in the ignition to listen to the radio.

I hopped across the muddy driveway, ran into a side door and down the polished hall. Laughing to myself, I opened the door to the children's ward.

There were rows of cribs and beds in the half-darkened room. I looked up and down the rows, but from where I stood, I couldn't see Baby in any of them.

Then in the farthest corner, beside the half-closed drapes, I saw Elsie and Mayva Potts. They were dressed in splendid flowery dresses, and I understood by their regal manner that they were on one of their Christian visitations to the less fortunate. They had with them a tiny figure whose face was as small and pale as a dime.

I saw it was Baby. They had Baby on Elsie's lap.

I ran to the corner where they were.

'Baby, it's me,' I said, leaning down to her, taking her arm, 'Baby, I'm here.'

Baby didn't move or look at me. Then she pulled the slightest bit closer to Elsie's flowery bosom.

'Come on, Baby, it's time to go home,' I said, reaching under her arms to lift her.

Baby's body went rigid, her arms clamped tighter around Elsie, her head still pressed between Elsie's breasts.

I began to pry Baby's white-tipped fingers, one by one, from Elsie's soft back and shoulders. Baby screamed as if cut with a knife.

Mayva stood, then stooped low to hold Baby and smooth her hair.

'Baby-girl, Baby-girl,' Mayva said.

Finally, breathless, I managed to lift Baby away, then held her to myself. Baby clung to me at last, her arms and legs fastened to me like vines. Her face breathed hot into the crook of my neck.

Mayva untied Baby's hospital gown and helped me dress Baby in the pants and shirt my mother'd sent. The shirt was hard to get on and we had to pull Baby's hands briefly off me to get her arms into the sleeves. Baby cried each time, then clung back to me.

Elsie reached into her mother's purse and brought out a dancing girl – a doll with a skirt made of red felt circles crimped and pleated and pinned together with red sequins. The skirts of such a doll could accordion out to hide something – a box of Kleenex or a roll of toilet paper.

Baby grabbed the dancing girl, then reattached to me.

I looked at the doll, its red skirt, its glittering sequins.

The doll wasn't that great, I thought. I'd seen the plastic bodies for such dolls in cellophane bags on Mayva's kitchen counter. She ordered them by the half-dozen. And the sequins which shone like rubies weren't really rubies. They were only tiny bits of coloured foil. I bet it was easy to make such a doll, I told myself. I bet I could do it if I tried.

I turned, and walked out of the room, Baby on my hip, the dancing girl pressed between us.

I squished through the mud to my dad's car, and got into the middle of the back seat with Baby.

Our dad started the motor and pulled away, slooshing mud

toward Mayva and Elsie who'd followed us out to the drive-way.

As we pulled away, Baby started to laugh, an almost silent laugh, which she hid in the glittering skirts of the dancing girl.

'Three cheers for the queen,' Elsie called, not stepping back from the splashing mud, 'All hail to the queen of the land.'

The centre of my chest ached as if bruised by a stone. I tried to ease the doll from Baby's grip, but she wouldn't let go. I tried to move it to the side, so it wouldn't poke into me, but Baby's hand wouldn't budge. She couldn't stop laughing.

Baby felt different. Her little giggling body felt lighter than a pin, but there was some new resistance in it. Her face looked different too. It was pale and secretive, a slightly waxy white, like the potatoes we'd grown in the bush.

We'd stumbled upon our garden last fall, and I'd been surprised to see one potato still growing there. It was long and spindly, a vine almost, but recognizably a potato.

I pulled it up and Elsie and Baby and I dug into the dirt with our fingers, squabbling a little over a fair division of space. Finally we found one, then two, then five potatoes quietly growing there.

Two were the size of crab-apples, and three the size of our fingernails. We scrubbed them off on our clothes and held them up to admire them.

My mother was wrong. It seemed almost impossible to believe, then, or even now, holding Baby on the way home from the hospital.

My mother was wrong.

This seemed as remarkable a thing as the potatoes themselves. Mama said we couldn't grow potatoes in the bush, but we did. We grew five of them.

I pulled Baby closer to me in the car, smelling her pale hair and the skin of her arm. Baby, her small body still vibrating with jerky laughter, didn't smell like Baby. She smelled of bandages and something metallic like rust.

I bent sideways, studied what I could see of Baby's face, then took my chance.

'I love you,' I said into her ear. 'I love you, Baby. Do you love me?'

'Ha-ha-ha-ha,' Baby answered. She was laughing in a staccato way now, almost as if she had hiccups. 'Ha-ha-ha-ha.' She still had her fingers laced through the skirt of the dancing girl, and pinched almost painfully onto the skin of my arm. I pressed my face into Baby's sweet stringy hair, and listened to the mud splashing up on one side and the other.

It was spring.

You could wear shoes outside.

There was nice music on the radio.

Potatoes grew.

Baby was out. Baby was out. Baby was out.

Eclipse

WHEN I GOT UP from the too-wide bed I used to share with Baby and went to the kitchen, my father was wearing a suit. It was a dark brown wool suit, and it was pulled snug over his shoulders and buttoned tight across his chest. In the suit, he looked important, almost English. In the suit, he looked like someone else.

I sat down beside my brother, Amel, who was still in his underwear at the far end of the table, watching.

'Where's Daddy going, Mama?' I asked my mother who was already at the frying pan.

Mama placed two fried eggs and two strips of bacon in front of Daddy and smiled in a strained way, as if he was a salesman or a minister.

'Where's Daddy going? Where's Daddy going?' she mimicked, still holding her brittle smile. Then she stopped smiling and turned to me. 'If you want to know so bad, why don't you ask. Ask him who's so fancy he needs to go there with a suit on. Ask who that Someone-Oh-So-Special is. Go ahead. Ask.' Then she stood and watched.

I wrapped my arms around myself because it was still cool in the kitchen.

'Where are you going, Daddy?' I asked.

My father finished his cup of coffee, then put the cup on the table, his hand still on the handle. My mother refilled it and we watched as he added a teaspoon of sugar and a dribble of evaporated milk, clinked a spoon in the cup, then lifted it to his mouth again.

'Where are you going in that suit, Daddy?' I asked again.

My father stood, checked the corners of his mouth for crumbs, then went out to the blue Dodge which waited in front of the house.

We followed as he got into the car, started the motor and drove away. We stood in a ragged line on the road and watched while the car drove across the bridge, past the dairy, then gathered speed as it passed the Ukrainian graveyard just outside of town.

The road turned left then, but we continued to watch while the cloud of dust rose, then dispersed. After that, there was only the grey strip of road, the clutter of town, the green fields beyond, and the radiant blue morning sky.

'Maybe he's gone and left us,' Mama said, her eyes dark. 'Maybe he's gone for good this time. Should I call the police?'

Amel picked up a rock and threw it down the road in the direction the car had gone.

'He went fishing!' Amel said.

'Why would he dress like that to go fishing?' Mama asked, looking closely at Amel to see if he knew something.

'He's testing the tires!' Amel said, tears running down his face.

We went inside the yard and stood a while in the garden. Everything was just starting to grow. At the back fence, the bright green peas were climbing the sticks Baby and I had pushed in for them. Near the shed, the carrots and garlic were a green fuzz. To one side of the house was a small field of potatoes, already a couple of inches high.

My mother stood with us, then turned abruptly, flaring out her orange and green skirt. She went to the shed and brought out a long-handled axe, then sat down on the back steps, her hair scooped up into a white bandana, her bare feet braced apart. She spat on one side of the blade and rubbed it with a stone, then did the same with the other side.

She tested the blade with her thumb. Then she took the axe, walked to the far side of the garden beyond the potatoes, and went directly to a poplar tree. The tree, which was over a foot thick at its base, was partly in our yard and partly in the neighbours'.

Without looking up at the tree, my mother lifted her axe and began chopping at the rough grey bark, aiming just below waist-level. The chopping had a hollow inconsequential sound, as if a child was banging on a fence post with a broomstick.

After some time, Dillard Dixon appeared from his house on the other side of the tree. His face was still fat with sleep and he carried a cup of coffee.

'What gives, Wilma?' he said in his squeaky, almost comical voice. 'What the heck is going on?' He looked at Mama, the axe, the tree, and at Amel and me still watching from behind the house.

Mama didn't stop to answer him.

'That tree shades this here porch,' Dillard said, raising his voice to be heard above the chopping. 'I don't mind that tree, Wilma. I don't mind it one bit.'

Our mother lowered the axe and rested its blade on the ground in front of her. She wiped under her eyes with the back of her hand and then pointed to the garden.

'Look,' she said. 'It's killing my potatoes.'

The potato leaves, for about thirty feet around the tree, were slightly smaller and a little more yellowish in colour.

Dillard came closer and stared around at the potatoes as if he'd never seen potatoes growing before. Finally he tipped his coffee on the ground.

'Leave her be, Wilma,' he said. 'I'll talk to Gilbert tonight. If you still want, maybe we'll take her down come Sunday. But leave her for now.'

Mama positioned both hands on the axe handle, braced her feet and continued chopping.

* * *

When Baby'd come home from the hospital in spring, she'd been better for a while. She crayoned people with hands like suns on the backs of old envelopes, cut pictures from the cata- logue, and dressed the cat in a red velvet doll's dress.

Then one Thursday after school I sat on the couch cutting out Dale Evans paper dolls, Baby's head on a pillow beside me. Baby's breath got quieter and quieter, as if she was falling asleep. Then her breath seemed to stop altogether.

I finished folding back the tabs of Dale Evans' white and gold rodeo skirt, and listened for Baby to start breathing. I cut out Dale Evans' white cowgirl hat with the gold star on front, put it on her, then walked Dale Evans across the arm of the couch. I looked at Baby again.

'Stop it, Baby,' I said, then walked Dale Evans down to the cushions of the couch. 'Stop fooling around, Baby.' I walked Dale Evans up Baby's arm and shoulder.

Then I ran for my mother.

My mother went for Dillard next door.

'Baby's dead,' she said.

'We got everything under control here,' Dillard said. 'We got everything under tight control.' And he drove Mama and Baby to the hospital.

In the empty house where I waited, the radio kept playing, the announcer kept dedicating songs, the afternoon sun kept slanting in through the window. Outside, the birds kept flying. White butterflies wobbled across the fence. The tree rustled prettily in the breeze. I saw all this with my own eyes. Nothing faltered, not even for a second.

I thought something should happen. I thought there should be an earthquake. I thought there should be an eclipse.

After the funeral, I dreamed of Baby. I dreamed Baby was behind the iron grate in the hot-air pipe from the furnace. The dream seemed so real that when I woke, I checked the dust in the mouth of the pipe for signs Baby really had been there.

Another time, dropping off to sleep, I heard Baby laugh.

After that, I had no dreams at all, not of Baby or of anything else.

* * *

The sun moved up, then overhead, and Amel and I moved

onto the back steps which still had some shade. Our mother came in and filled a jar of water which she drank at once. She tore strips of cloth from an old white sheet and bandaged her hands. Then she went back to the tree.

'I saw where he went once!' Amel said suddenly, his face still puffy and smudged from crying. 'McCue's pasture!'

'Daddy?' I said. 'Was someone with him? Was a lady with him?'

There was the steady sound of chopping from the side of the yard again.

'He was in the car. Just sitting there with the windows rolled up. Let's go see if he's there. We could look for clues.'

'We better look here first,' I said. I knew about detective work from the Dick Tracy comics.

We looked first at the still uncleared breakfast table.

'Don't touch anything,' Amel said, starting to cheer up.

Our father had eaten everything off his plate and had polished it as usual with a crust of toast.

In our parents' bedroom, there was only the neatly made bed, the eyes that followed us from the pictures on the wall, and the smell of flour from the flour bin which was stored behind the bedroom door.

The cardboard clicker on Amel's bicycle spokes had fallen off and I had to wait for him to repair it. Then we rode out across the bridge.

'Your Daddy sick? Where's your Daddy?' Old Man Coons hollered at us, waving his cane.

Amel clicked right past, pretending not to hear.

I cleared my throat politely as I pedalled.

We rode past the sign at the edge of town, and past the Ukrainian graveyard. I couldn't look at Baby's grave, now heaped high with plastic flowers. I couldn't look away from it either.

The graveyard was a flat field enclosed by a barbed-wire fence. There were only a few graves along one end. Almost all of it was still tall, dusty grass. In the middle was an eastern style cross with white peeling paint. On three sides was Hal Holldorson's hay field. Beyond that, bush.

When we got to the hill that dipped down to McCue's pasture, we saw no one, not our father, not his car, not even any of the McCues or the McCue cows. Only a few crows rose from the bush beside the creek, then sifted down on the trees again.

Amel and I left our bikes in the ditch beside the bullet-pocked *No-Trespassing-And-That-Means-You* sign, and followed the foot trail to the creek.

'Caw!' hollered a crow behind us, and we jumped, then laughed.

We had our feet in the stony creek when the gun exploded.

I thought I'd been shot. But when I felt my chest and arms, I found I was all right. Then I thought Amel'd been shot.

The gun sounded close by, again, then again.

Amel and I crouched, and ran into the trees. Silence, then another gunshot.

Finally, through the trees, I saw who was shooting. It was Old Man McCue. He was aiming the rifle in our direction, but above our heads. He's shooting crows, I thought.

Then I looked up and saw what he was aiming at – an orange forestry plane flying over his barley field to the south.

As we watched he shot again, reloaded, and took aim again.

The orange plane continued steadily across the blue sky. It looked like it was made of balsa wood.

Amel and I, crouching, made our way back to our bikes, then pedalled in the direction of home as fast as we could. Behind us, the gun sounded once more, then once more again.

'Look!' Amel yelled. 'A clue!' He pointed to an empty vodka bottle in the dust at the side of the road.

'That's dumb,' I said, without stopping or slowing down. 'That's plain pitiful.'

I wouldn't wait for him and Amel trailed behind, crying aloud as he pedalled.

At home, our mother was still chopping the tree. The sound of the axe seemed louder now, and the leaves of the poplar trembled lightly in the breeze.

Near Mama in the garden I saw what looked for a moment like a scarecrow. It was the Nazarene minister, a small, thin, blotchy-faced man, dressed entirely in baggy black clothes, except for his white collar. He looked like a child dressed up in his father's clothes.

'Not a-one of us can understand the ways of God,' he said to Mama, straining to be heard above the chopping. 'I swear I don't understand a half of what I see.'

Mama stopped for a moment. 'I could break stones,' she said, and lifted her axe again.

A few minutes later she paused, looked up at the tree, changed her angle, and chopped from the other side.

The black-suited Nazarene minister stepped backward, forward, backward and forward again. Then he made his way through the potatoes to where I was standing with Amel and moved us to beyond the back steps where we were further from the tree.

The tree continued to stand, then without warning, swayed slightly. Suddenly it passed across the sky like the wing of an enormous bird.

I grabbed onto the black sleeve of the Nazarene minister's jacket, expecting the tree to slam hard against the ground, but when it landed, it came down almost lightly, with only a rushing of leaves, and the snapping of a few branches.

I walked over to where the tree lay broken across the field of potatoes, its green skirts curtained around it. I kicked at the branches, tore handfuls of leaves from it, and shredded the leaves in my hands.

'See?' I said to it. 'See?'

The trunk of the tree near the top was as smooth and cool as skin.

We heard the gate click, which meant the black-suited

minister had gone home, and we went in. We ate boiled eggs and bread with jam, then went to bed. Through my bedroom window I saw that the sun was down, but the sky still held the light.

In the morning, I woke early. In my sleep, I'd seen cups. Then, from the kitchen, I heard the clink of cups. I heard my mother talking to someone in Ukrainian. Then I heard the other voice. It was my father.

I got up and went to the kitchen.

My dad sat behind the table, unshaven, his suit jacket unbuttoned now, and wrinkled. He smelled of sweat and motor oil.

On the table was a dusty cellophane bag of Christmas candy, and a fuzzy moose that said *Souvenir of Canada*.

'Here I am, going half crazy,' Mama shouted, switching to English when she saw me. 'Is he dead? Is he in a car crash? Is he lying in a ditch somewhere? Is he in jail? Did someone shoot him?' She stood beside the stove, tears running down her face now, her hands still bandaged with torn strips of white cloth. 'What makes you think you can come crawling back here like some old tomcat?'

She turned to me. 'You want to know where your father was? Go ahead! Ask him! Ask him! He went to see Annie Karachuk, his old girlfriend!'

Daddy stood up and cleared his throat. I thought of the time I'd seen him throw the handful of dirt into Baby's grave. I thought of the time I'd seen him cry.

He stood there a moment. When he spoke his voice was hoarse.

'You,' he said to Mama in English. 'You. You.'

He took a step toward my mother. Then he did something I'd never seen anyone do before. He knelt before my mother, raised her bandaged hands, one at a time, and pressed them to his lips.

World Fair

I WAS CHALKING a hopscotch on the sidewalk when I saw my brother, Amel, down the street by the bus depot. He was walking with someone that looked like our dad. Their outlines shimmered in the heat, and I thought for a moment that they might vanish completely, like a mirage of water on the highway.

As I watched, the man and Amel became closer and more substantial. Amel was towing the man as if by an invisible string, and as they approached, I saw the man really was our dad, not someone else at all.

'We're going to the World Fair,' I heard Amel say to Fred-the-Barber who sat on his front steps. 'We're going to the Seattle World Fair.'

'That's nice, sonny,' Fred-the-Barber said. 'You don't say.' He looked curiously at our dad.

'Kids!' our dad said, grinning. He clamped his mouth shut to adjust his teeth and grinned again.

Amel and my dad walked straight past me to the backyard where my mother was hanging washing on the clothesline.

'Oh!' my mother said, almost dropping a sheet into the cabbages that grew by the back steps. My dad hardly ever came home in the middle of the day, only when he got his teeth pulled out, or when Old Man Krueger fell down dead chalking his pool cue. Daddy was home on Sundays, of course, but we were used to that. On Sundays he slept on the couch or whittled wood in the shed.

'You can't go just like that,' my mother said, frowning. She reached into her apron pocket for a clothespin. 'You need reservations. They said on the radio. You need tickets. Who knows what all. You can't just pick up like King Toot.'

The far end of the clothesline squealed as she reeled it out, pinning up a sheet.

The wash was hung in this order: sheets, towels, men's shirts, women's dresses, children's clothing, men's pants. Largest to smallest and lightest to darkest. Socks and underwear were hung on a small line less visible from the road.

Daddy pushed up the peak of his olive-green cap with one finger.

'A man's word is law,' he said. 'You say something, you got to do it.' He grinned at Amel who was watching without a sound.

'Get in the car,' our dad said, speaking loudly and pointing to the road to give his voice authority.

'I'm not going anywhere,' our mother said, hanging on to the clothesline with one hand. 'What about the poolroom? You can't walk off just like that.' She held her other hand up against the sun to look at our dad.

Daddy just stood there in his dark, baggy clothes. The peak of his cap shielded his eyes from the sun. He said nothing.

'At least let me run the poolroom for you,' our mother said. 'Keep it open. It's bad for business to close it down. I could make a few dollars of my own.'

I pulled grasses from along the fence, pulling each one carefully so that it detached, revealing a tender white stalk that was good to chew.

It's funny, I thought. Why is a shoe called shoe? Why not mud? Why is mud called mud? Why not bottle or boxcar?

I balanced on one leg, chewing my grass. I went to my mother.

'Come with us, Mama,' I said.

'In the middle of washing clothes? Are you crazy?' our mother said. 'And what about the garden?'

'We'll be back in a few days,' our dad said. 'Four, five, six outside. What does it matter,' he grinned to Amel. 'We answer to no one.'

Amel smiled at this.

I traced a design on the ground with the toe of my shoe.

My mother began to cry, choked, almost silent weeping which she made no attempt to hide. She bent down, picked up a blue shirt from the plastic tub, shook it out. A shower of water pellets hit my arm. They were sharp as sand.

* * *

When our mother came home from the hospital last time, she talked fast, not looking at anyone, tripping over herself to explain all the things that'd happened to her.

She talked about the woman in the next bed who crocheted pot holders, a different design every day, sometimes apple, sometimes pear, occasionally pineapple. The pineapple took the longest.

She told us how she'd sometimes been given the flowers of other patients who'd been discharged, once blue hydrangeas, as big as grapefruits.

She tried out hospital recipes on us, mashed potato and hamburger casseroles with corn flakes on the top, green Jell-O with grated carrot suspended in it, even boiled raisins.

I tried to act interested in the hospital stories and to eat the boiled raisins, at least I did at first. It was like a test at school, with the lights too bright, no looking at the other papers, and an occasional trick question.

'That woman,' I said. 'Did she follow the same pattern all the time or what?'

'You don't really want to know,' my mother said, throwing her dishrag into the pan. 'I told you that already.'

Amel and I would come home from school and find our mother washing the floor and crying, peeling potatoes and crying, hanging on to the doorframe and crying.

Never, I told myself. Never, never, never.

* * *

We helped our dad load the blue Dodge with two brown-paper shopping bags of clothes, a pickle jar of water, and a box of Sweet Maries from my dad's stock of chocolate bars for the poolroom.

Daddy and Amel climbed into the front, and I went into the back seat of the car. Daddy slammed the door twice, revved the motor to check it out, and pulled onto the road.

Suddenly my mother ran out of the house in a straight, quick line, her hair streaming out of one side of her bandana. She stopped at the edge of the sidewalk and screamed after us, 'Big shot! Big shot! Big shot!'

I checked the street in both directions, to see who might have heard. My dad and Amel stared straight ahead. The car did not alter its speed.

Even when night fell, my dad kept driving. Sometime during the night he pulled off the road. Neither Amel nor I could sleep, what with the exitement, and the mosquitoes that found us even with the windows rolled up.

Our dad tried to sleep in the trunk, and the car heaved frequently as he changed position. After various adjustments, crashing back and forth into the bush, and some swearing, he gave up on sleeping, got back behind the wheel, and pulled back onto the highway.

It was light enough to see pine trees, grey rock and turquoise lakes through the low white mist.

I said laundry blueing must have been put in the water, and Amel said that was stupid and we argued dispiritedly.

I wanted to sit in the front.

'There's no room,' Amel said.

'No room,' my dad agreed, crouching over the wheel. He made it a point to drive with one hand only, to let no one pass us, and was beginning to show the strain.

'There's lots of room up front,' I said. 'Look.'

'No, there's not,' my dad and Amel countered. Amel rocked his outspread knees to demonstrate.

'You've got the whole back seat to yourself,' my dad said.

I wished my mother was like mothers I'd read about in books, who would come on trips, sing songs, pass sandwiches, and let me have a turn in the front.

When we stopped for breakfast, I refused to eat.

For lunch, I would only eat pie.

'Bloody pie,' I said. 'Bloody restaurant,' 'Bloody car,' and 'Bloody sun.' Back in the moving car, I said, 'Bloody road,' and my dad flailed back with his free arm, trying to hit me.

In the Fraser Valley, our dad pulled over to pick up a soldier who was standing by the road with his thumb up and a cardboard sign saying, 'SEATTLE OR BUST'.

We stopped at Hell's Gates and the soldier stood a while on the lookout.

The soldier explained the pin on his cap to Amel, who kept turning around to look at it. He told us how he'd worn a brand new suit his first day in the army and how they'd made him clean toilets all day in it.

At the border we had to get out of the car, even the soldier. Privately, I blamed this on my father. I noticed he smiled too much, then hesitated and looked sideways when they asked the purpose of our visit.

When we reached Seattle, it took half the night to find a motel room. The one we took had two beds, a TV, a shower and a toilet.

The soldier said, well, maybe he should be heading on, but my dad said only a crazy man would refuse the opportunity to sleep on the floor.

One of the beds had a machine that vibrated the bed for a quarter, but it didn't work, and didn't return the quarter.

In the morning, to open the door, we had to peel up the corner of the carpet.

*　*　*

These were the things that happened at the Seattle World Fair:

1. Our arms, upon admission, were stamped with an invisible

ink. We were then required to stand under a special light, and the outline of the Seattle Space-Needle glowed electric blue from the skin of our arms.

2. We learned to call everything by another name, Heloport, Bubbleator, The World of Tomorrow, Utopia Fries, Futuria Burgers.

3. We rode the monorail which travelled from the Space Needle into the city and back. It was the transportation of the future. If you touched the rail you would be electrocuted.

4. At the Seattle Space Needle, I bought a plastic orange ballpoint shaped like the Space Needle.

5. We were told by a lady in pink about the revolving restaurant at the top of the Space Needle. The lady had put her purse on the window ledge, and it had disappeared, then returned three hours later.

6. We went up the Bubbleator to The World of Tomorrow. We saw a midget come out of the men's toilet. He was smaller than Amel, but wore men's suspenders.

7. Amel and I saw a demonstration of a special device that cut vegetables into various fancy shapes. Potato chips could be zigzagged, or slices of carrot cut into butterfly shapes. We pooled $4.89, and bought one for our mother.

8. The soldier took us on the triple ferris wheel. He'd disappeared the first day at the Space Needle, then reappeared the third night in the motel room, with a swollen eye and a peacock feather.

9. I threw up on the ferris wheel.

10. The soldier paid a dollar to shoot at a paper bull's eye with a rifle riveted to a metal post. He won a goldfish in a plastic bag of water, gave the paper bull's eye to Amel, and the fish in the bag of water to me. The fish shone gold and silver, as if lit from within. Its eyes were perfectly black and round, like decals.

* * *

Every night we returned to our motel room for supper, which was pink and white marshmallow cookies. Amel and I watched TV, and our dad drank whisky from a water glass.

On the morning of our fourth day at the Fair, Daddy woke up tired and wanting to go home. Amel took the soap from the motel room, but our dad said he couldn't take the ashtrays or the picture of the sailing ship.

'Leave that fish here,' our dad said. 'It'll die.'

Within half an hour he'd paid our bill and we were back in the car looking for the road to the highway north.

Between my feet, I held a paper bag with a jar of water and the fish in it. Occasionally a little water sloshed through the bottom of the bag.

We drove straight back, stopping only for gas, and at the border, where I hid the jar under my skirt.

After the border, my dad put his teeth in a bread bag, and put them on the dash. He kept his free hand on the shoulder of the arm he used to steer with. Amel slept in the front seat beside him.

I sat in the centre of the back seat, watching the silver and blue pools of water on the road appear and vanish. Through the paper bag, I could feel the glass jar that contained my prize. I noticed how the clouds and fields, the road, the car, our very selves were arranged of crystals of colour and watery light.

Look how bright we shine, I thought. Look how lightly we fly across the long, straight road, sometimes not seeming to touch the ground at all.

City Slickers

AUNTIE ROSE's new husband was a real catch. Tall, dark and handsome, Rose promised in her letters and sent pictures to prove it. When Auntie Rose and our new uncle Dez arrived on the 8 a.m. bus, everyone talked at once.

'If a man is hungry,' my father pronounced in ringing tones, 'let him eat!'

'Maybe you won't like this,' my mother said, shuffling to the table with two plates of sausages and eggs. 'Maybe I didn't cook it right.'

'How many city slickers to change a lightbulb?' my brother Amel asked, as my dad directed Rose and Dez to their chairs. 'One to hold the lightbulb and one to call the electrician!'

Our dad laughed out loud, looking over to Dez to invite him to join in, and Uncle Dez smiled politely around the table, then reached over to ruffle Amel's blond hair.

Uncle Dez's hands, I noticed, were narrow, the fingers long and tapered at the tips, not square-tipped, like my dad's. He was tall and good-looking, though the curves of his face were the slightest bit smoothed out, as if he'd been carved of soap, then used once or twice to wash with. He wore tan-coloured pants and shirt, the shirt squared with creases, as though it'd been pulled fresh from its package.

Yellow-haired Rose shone up at us and held out her left hand for us to see. A diamond glittered from her ring finger. Dez turned to her and kissed her lightly on the lips.

We stared and grinned, not used to diamonds, not used to kissing. We were pleased and embarrassed, but too interested to look away.

Rose's cheeks were pink and she looked pretty in a yellow sundress and matching bolero jacket, the diamond sparking like fire crackers as she buttered her toast.

I was dressed up for the occasion of their visit too. I wore an ensemble I'd sewn in Home Ec, a gathered skirt with a printed pattern of horses and hounds around the bottom, and a green peasant blouse.

'So,' my dad said. 'You ever been up in this part of the country?' *Cown-try* is what he said. My dad was self-taught in English and sometimes pronounced words the way they were spelled.

'Here's the salt,' my dad said. 'You like pepper?' The rest of us had eaten earlier while we were waiting. Uncle Dez tried to swallow and my dad shifted his chair closer in a friendly way. 'You like it here? Or maybe you like it better in the city?'

'City people like to brag they got a house in the country,' my mother said. 'Well, I guess we can brag too. We already live here.' And she looked up at Uncle Dez and smiled in a shame faced way while my dad and Amel laughed out loud again.

Uncle Dez smiled, revealing teeth of an uneven yellow colour. 'It's very beautiful here,' he said. 'The trees, the rivers. When we were on the bus, we saw the sun rise. Rose pointed out a moose, standing at the side of the road. It was very striking.'

We beamed, happy to have pleased him with our trees and rivers, our sunrise, our moose.

'Lesee,' my dad said then, squinting sideways as if lining up balls on a pooltable. 'Lesee now. You're in dentist school along with the other dentists, that-a-right?'

'He *was*,' my mother said, leaning over to my dad. 'He was in dentist school. I *told* you. He's *not* in dentist school anymore. He only *was*.'

'It was gruelling work,' Auntie Rose said brightly. 'Gruelling!'

'You're quite right, Rose,' Uncle Dez said, frowning thoughtfully, resting the tips of his knife and fork on his plate.

'Rose is right, of course. The work has its own reward, naturally enough. But I prefer, for the present, to pursue other contacts.'

He smelled so nice and was so polite, I felt sorry for him having to answer all my dad's questions. I'd been disappointed about dentist school too, but it seemed better than not having gone at all. Just think, I said to myself, I have an uncle who's been to dental college.

'A dentist,' my dad explained, 'he gets to call his own shots. You go somewhere else, you might not be so well off.'

I was embarrassed by how my family was acting, my father thinking the louder the better and grilling Uncle Dez about dental school, my mother sweating and ground-down-looking, and Amel under the pathetic delusion that any idiot thing that passed through his head was funny.

Even our house, I could see, was wrong – the bare table top with a few crumbs from our earlier breakfast, the evaporated milk can with two holes punched into the lid, all of us crowded around like a tribe of capturing cannibals. I babysat for people on the other side of town and knew that people like Uncle Dez were accustomed to things I'd seen there – split-level homes, matched furniture, swag lamps artfully hung from the ceilings by chains.

'Each man marches to a different drummer,' I burst out. 'Not everybody needs to be a dentist.'

Uncle Dez paused, then turned to me. 'Well said, Irene,' He looked at me intently. 'That's very astute. Very astute indeed.'

My cheeks burned hot and the room seemed to darken slightly, then go brighter than before. I pulled at the elastic neckline of my blouse to let in a cooling breeze. The blouse was supposed to have a low neckline that ruffled gracefully across the shoulders, but mine fit snugly around the throat. I forgot my elastic the day we did necklines and had to make do with what my friends would give me.

Astute. I stored the word away in my head to look up as soon as I had a chance. It was a word we'd done in Vocabulary at school, but the force of the compliment knocked its meaning completely from my head.

'I got the boat on the car,' my dad said to Dez. 'I got the gear inside. Time to go fishing. You. Me. Amel.'

Then, from somewhere, a bottle appeared in his hand and my dad was pouring something gold into mustard glasses, one for Uncle Dez and another for himself.

'One for the road,' he said, raising his glass in a toast.

There was a lull, then my mother, smiling because of the guests, spoke up. 'Why do you need that?' she said.

She turned to Uncle Dez. 'I'm always scared,' she said, hunching down and twisting at her skirt. 'I'm always scared he's going to fall out of the boat and drown.'

My dad and Amel laughed out loud, then finally, as if dragged in against her will, my mother joined in and laughed along in her own shame faced way.

I sat as if made of stone. They were talking and laughing in one big mish-mash instead of taking turns the way I knew you were supposed to. And they were laughing about stupid things, city slicker jokes and about falling out of boats. These weren't things city people would laugh about, I thought. Not city people like my new Uncle Dez.

I looked over at Uncle Dez. He was standing beside his half-eaten breakfast with the grave, attentive look of someone listening to a distant train. My father downed his drink and slammed the glass onto the table in a way my mother would not normally tolerate.

'It's such a beautiful day,' Rose said, smiling and passing Uncle Dez a lit cigarette. 'What could be nicer than this fresh country air and summer sunshine? Who could ask for more than their own health on a day like this?'

My mother leaned over and jerked on my father's sleeve to get his attention.

'It's not like the Old Country,' she stage-whispered to him. 'You don't have to force liquor on your guests the minute they put their foot in the door. You don't have to force liquor at all.'

'Oh, it's going to be heaven out there on the lake today,' Rose said.

'What sort of fish do you have here?' Uncle Dez asked, ignoring his untouched drink and focusing tight in on Amel. 'Rainbow trout? Perch? Salmon?'

'Sure, we got salmon,' Amel yelped back. 'How many cans do you want?'

'What a joker!' my dad laughed as he led the way to the car, Amel and Uncle Dez close behind. 'What a joker! You got many jokers like that in dentist school?'

* * *

Astute. I read the definition quickly, not wanting my mother to see me looking up the word in the dictionary.

Mentally penetrating, the entry read, *gifted with discernment, practically wise, exceptionally intelligent*. The molecules of air beat against my eardrums. I slammed the dictionary shut and shoved it back on the shelf.

I looked into the mirror where I was afraid I'd see the same broad-boned, suntanned face, a variation of my mother's, look back at me. But this time, looking sideways into the dresser mirror with a smaller hand mirror, I thought I glimpsed a hint of something different. There, on the curve of my eyebrow, wasn't there the suggestion of discernment? And there, in the line of my jaw, especially if I sucked in my cheeks, I detected a certain quick intelligence.

It felt good to be astute. It felt taller, more spacious, more connected. I liked it. I liked the clear-eyed ruthless feel of it.

In the kitchen, my mother and Auntie Rose were talking.

'I never know,' I heard Auntie Rose say. 'I never know from one day to the next, or one hour to the next.'

'Most men drink too much until they settle down,' my mother answered. 'Give him some time to come to his senses.'

Rose was wiping her eye with a Kleenex when I came in.

'A speck in my eye,' she said, smiling at me.

'I hope Uncle Dez is having fun,' I said, wanting to work his name into the conversation. I still had the airy feeling that came with the knowledge of my astuteness.

Auntie Rose flicked her lighter to light a cigarette.

'Don't be discouraged by the difficulties in life, Irene,' she said. 'Don't look on the dark side.' She fit the lighter into its spot in her gold cigarette case and snapped it shut. Now that the men were gone, she was wearing green and white striped shorts and top, which made her eyes look green instead of blue.

'When I was young,' she said to my mother, 'I thought I was so damn smart.'

'Sit still,' my mother said, dangling a needle on a long thread over Auntie Rose's stomach. 'I'll tell you if you're having a boy or a girl.'

Auntie Rose raised her cigarette so as not to interfere with the swinging needle. We watched to see whether the needle would settle into a circular shape for a girl, or a back and forth pattern for a boy.

The needle circled and swung above the green and white stripes, then suddenly, before the needle had a chance to settle, Rose pushed the needle aside with the back of her hand. She counted a moment on her fingers, then stood up to look at the calendar on the wall.

'No,' she said finally, cigarette smoke trailing up. 'No, thank heavens. I'm not even late. I'm pretty sure I don't have that to worry about.'

My mother bent over a dishtowel and ran the thread through, so as not to waste it, then stabbed the needle back into the pincushion. Her face had a closed-down look, as if she'd been slighted in some way.

'Well, it's no use moping around,' Rose said, crushing out her cigarette. 'I might as well do something.'

'Does Uncle Dez like saskatoons?' I asked.

'That's a good idea, Irene,' Auntie Rose said, getting up. 'Let's pick some saskatoons for supper. I know – let's make a saskatoon pie.'

'There's a can of cherry filling in the cupboard,' my mother said in a flat voice.

'No,' Rose said, getting out bowls to pick into. 'Let's make it from scratch, Irene.'

'Let's put a tablecloth on the table,' I said. In the new place I'd got to in my head, I was able to ignore my mother's sulking. 'Let's put flowers in the middle.'

* * *

'Home is the hunter, home from the hill,' Auntie Rose called out when we went to the front to meet the car. She was wearing the yellow sundress again, and yellow sling-backed pumps to match.

Uncle Dez unfolded himself from the car, and staring mostly at a spot a little to the side of her, handed Rose a fishing rod. She carried it back to the house, smiling steadily as if she was carrying a flag in a parade.

Uncle Dez's pants were rolled to mid-calf in a way I was surprised a man would be willing to do, openly exposing hairy, paper-white calves. I couldn't help staring. His rolled-up pants were wet at the bottoms, and smeared here and there with mud. A piece of lakeweed stuck to one of his toast-coloured socks.

My father brought the wooden crate of fish into the back yard and eased his wet shoes off.

'Well,' he said, rolling up his sleeves and wafting the smell of whisky around him. 'I caught seventeen. How many did you catch again there, Dez?'

'Three,' Amel said. 'I caught four and he caught three.'

'Oh, wonderful,' Rose said.

My dad slit a fish open and threw the entrails over the fence to the cats. He looked over to Uncle Dez who sat beside the bench on an upturned Coke crate.

'A guy, he's got to be in good shape to go fishing,' my dad said, dropping the filleting knife to the bench and crouching down in a warlike stance.

'Eyes!' he said, darting his slightly bloodshot eyes one way then the other. 'Ears!' He cupped a hand behind one ear. 'Hands!' And he chopped the air lightly three times to demonstrate the state of his reflexes.

'For gosh sakes,' my mother said, and started to scrape at the fish herself, sending fish scales spraying.

'We can feast on these for days,' Rose said, looking at the fish still in the crate.

Dez sat on the Coke crate without speaking. His hair was ruffled up in the middle like a rooster's comb, and his face was as pale as his calves, except for the sunburn on his nose, one side of his forehead, and under one eye.

'Oh, your poor neck,' Rose said, opening a blue jar of sunburn cream she'd got from the house. Dez recoiled slightly as she applied the cream.

'Maybe he's got sunstroke,' my mother said.

'Thank you,' Dez said, smiling at her with his slightly worn-down handsome look. 'Thank you, but I'm completely all right. I've had, perhaps, a bit too much sun.'

Then supper was ready, a cross-stitched tablecloth on the table, pink cosmos in the middle, paper serviettes which I'd bought in a last-minute trip to the store.

My mother served the fish from the frying pan. There were baby potatoes cooked in their skins, bright green peas, a lettuce and green onion salad.

'Eat now,' my mother urged, 'before it gets cold.'

My dad sat down beside Uncle Dez. I headed for the chair on the other side of Dez, but Amel got there first.

'Isn't this wonderful?' Rose said. 'Doesn't this fresh country air give you an appetite? I know it does me.'

'A man, if he doesn't do so good,' my dad said, 'he shouldn't worry. He might do better tomorrow.'

'Who cares,' my mother said. 'As long as there's fish, who cares who caught them?'

'That's right,' my dad said. 'It doesn't matter that one guy catches seventeen and the other guy catches five.'

'Three,' Amel said.

'That's right.'

'In Home Ec we had to make a peasant blouse,' I said. I wanted to side with Uncle Dez in the conversation. I wanted Dez to know I wasn't like my dad, who couldn't let go of how many fish, or how few, a person caught. 'Mrs Fenshaw said we had to put thirty-six inches of elastic into the neckline. I only put half of that, and she said it was wrong, but I think it turned out all right.' I pulled on the ruffled collar of my blouse, turning the top seam over so they could see where I'd put in the elastic.

I glanced at Uncle Dez, but he wasn't looking at the seam I was holding out. He was looking at a water glass of whisky that had appeared in front of his plate. There was another in front of my dad's plate.

'More potatoes?' Rose asked. 'Dez? Amel? They're delicious!'

'Take a taste,' my dad said, pushing his glass of whisky across the table to me.

I shook my head. I already knew the hot turpentine taste of whisky, and I had no desire to try it again.

Amel reached across Dez's plate, picked up my dad's glass, took a sip, then slammed the glass down, clutching dramatically at his throat, his face red, his tongue hanging out, his eyeballs rolling.

I pretended not to notice, but my dad laughed. Amel took another sip, choked again, and my dad laughed again, then took his drink back.

Uncle Dez wasn't watching Amel either. He was picking the fish skeleton up from his plate, holding it by one end. 'Alas, poor Yorick,' he said.

We stared at his fish bones.

'I've been meaning to ask you about this tooth,' my mother said, pointing to a tooth of hers near the back. 'Sometimes it aches, then the whole side of my head aches.'

'Drink!' my father roared. 'Drink!'

I felt a tiny red spark sizzle then explode inside my head,

'Why should he?' I said, my face flushing with anger and my own boldness. 'Why should he drink? Maybe there's more things to life than drinking.'

I looked over at my father's surprise. I hardly noticed the sound from across the table – something like a hiss, or the spitting noise a cat makes when its tail gets caught in the door.

'So!' Dez said, looking in my direction. His face was chalk white on one half, and bright red on the other half, with a few silvery fish scales glittering beside the ear on the red half. 'So! This one is ready to be a wife also!'

He glared at me, his face a mask of fury.

I was as shocked as if I'd been slapped.

My father ignored me. 'You're a man,' he said to Dez. 'You don't need to argue with nobody.'

'There's dessert!' Auntie Rose cried out, standing up. My mother stood too, and started to clear the plates.

Uncle Dez reached for his whisky and turned it around in his hands, as if admiring the swirl of the liquid against the glass. Then he raised his hand, and drank the whisky down like water.

'Irene and I made a saskatoon pie,' Rose said.

'I don't think they want pie now,' my mother said.

'You don't need to be mad at yourself,' my mother said to me when the men took their whisky into the front room. 'It's not like you poured it down his throat. It's not like anybody forced him.'

I didn't know what my mother was talking about. I didn't understand a single thing out of all the things that'd happened all day. I tried to trace back in my mind to find some connecting thread, but whichever thread I followed, I always arrived at what Dez had said, that grey lumpy knot, so big and unsightly and so hopelessly sewn into the fabric that it ruined the whole garment: *So. This one is ready to be a wife also.*

'You better eat up the pie,' my mother said, friendlier again now. She cut an enormous piece of pie and placed it in front of me.

I looked at the pie and thought how odd it was that men preferred whisky to pie. It felt like something I should have already known, like explaining about the blouse. Mrs Fenshaw had warned us against this, against listing the ingredients of a dish while people were eating it, or describing the difficulties of making a garment while we were wearing it. The trick was, she'd told us, to make it look easy. It was better simply to smile mysteriously, to keep people guessing. But I'd forgotten that piece of advice until now.

Amel staggered into the kitchen from the front room, pretending to have trouble following a black line on the linoleum.

'Woo-eee,' he said in a plaintive voice. 'Woo-eee, boy, am I drunk.'

My mother also cut him a large piece of pie and he sat down beside me and proceeded to mush it up with his fork the way he always did.

My mother turned to the sink and began to run water for the dishes. Rose sat at the table, folding and unfolding one of the paper serviettes.

'I would do anything for him,' Rose said, her napkin a worn fan now. 'I would go anywhere, I would be anything, but nothing I can do is enough.'

My mother turned around. 'Have a baby,' she said, her voice high and urgent, her soapy hands stretched out to Rose. 'What you need is a baby! Something to take care of!

Something to make a fuss about! He would have a reason to change if he had a son!'

I ate my pie in layers, the way I liked to, first the light sugary crust, then the sweet juicy filling, and finally the moist soft bottom crust which I picked up and ate with my fingers like a cookie.

Usually I couldn't stand it, the way Amel mushed his pie, but this time I was glad of his company. It was a relief not to have to explain anything, or use a fork every minute like you were supposed to.

I felt bruised and battered around on my back and shoulders, as if I'd pulled out on an elastic cord, then snapped back to where I was before.

My mother washed the dishes. Auntie Rose dried. Amel and I sat side by side, our shoes just touching, and finished our pie without speaking.

The Short-Wave Radio

OUR MOTHER AND FATHER promised my brother, Amel, a short-wave radio when the results of his provincial exams came in and it was official that he had passed grade ten.

'It's the one in Jack-the-Jeweller's window,' my dad said. He was standing beside the kitchen table, holding his electric shaver, which was already plugged in in the bathroom. 'You think you can order a radio like that from the hardware? You can't! You have to order a radio like that from the jewellery store!'

I leaned my free elbow on the table and tried to settle my attention on my corn flakes and milk. Within minutes my friend Leigh-Ann was picking me up to walk to the hospital where we both had summer jobs.

Amel was eating his corn flakes with bananas and cream from a mixing bowl. In the past year, Amel had grown a foot taller, had developed a broad back and wide shoulders. Even the bones in his face had shifted slightly, leaving him movie-star handsome.

'Nice wood cabinet,' my dad added, 'light-up dial, three knobs underneath. When you're tired of studying, son, you can listen to the radio for a while.' My dad switched on his shaver, then stepped back in front of the bathroom mirror.

Our mother and father had plans for Amel. They planned he would finish high school and go to university in the city where he would become a druggist. Counting out pills was a clean, steady job, they reasoned, practically as good as a doctor, but with not nearly the same schooling required.

Amel reached for the pancake syrup with his long, muscular arm, swirled the syrup over his corn flakes, and kept on eating.

I pushed back my chair and pulled a bottle of liquid shoe-polish from the pocket of my yellow hospital uniform. I dipped the fuzzy ball into the bottle and bent over to smear the chalky polish onto the scuffed white oxfords I was wearing.

'When you pass grade twelve, son,' my dad said, shutting off the shaver, 'I'll buy you one of those plug-in vibrating chairs so that you can sit and listen to the radio on it.'

I pictured Amel, wearing a white lab coat, sitting on his vibrating chair, listening to voices from Tokyo or Berlin, and heard a crackle in my brain like the static on a short-wave radio.

'Priceless,' I said, sitting up and flutter-kicking my feet to dry the polish. 'That's really priceless.'

My parents craned their necks in my direction. They looked slightly startled, as if something odd had happened. As if I'd suddenly started speaking in Greek, or announced I was flying to the moon.

'I passed grade ten last year and no one bought *me* a radio,' I said. 'No one offered *me* a vibrating chair. No one gave me so much as a c-card.'

Amel flipped a rat-tail comb through his Elvis Presley hair, cast his Jimmy Dean eyes briefly in my direction, then without saying anything, left for his job at Morf's Modern Motors.

'How's Amel?' Leigh-Ann said when she knocked on the door a moment later. 'Still eating?' She stepped in and examined the mixing bowl Amel'd eaten from.

Leigh-Ann was tall and blonde and had a horse named Roger that she rode every summer in the Stampede Parade.

I picked up my lunch and headed out with her. I didn't want to explain about the radio until we were out of ear-shot of the house and I could be sure of a sympathetic audience.

'You know what Amel's getting for passing grade ten?' I asked Leigh-Ann when we were out on the highway. The highway would take us past Morf's Modern Motors, and eventually, the hospital. It wasn't the only route, but according to Leigh-Ann, it was the best, on account of being most frequently graded and the best-gravelled.

'They're getting Amel a short-wave radio,' I said. 'You know what I got when I passed grade ten?' I linked my thumb and forefinger and held them up in a zero.

'You're kidding!' Leigh-Ann said, grinning and stopping in her tracks. 'A *short-wave radio?*'

'And me, nothing,' I prompted her.

Leigh-Ann steadied herself against me and dumped a piece of gravel from her shoe.

'It's in Jack-the-Jeweller's window,' I explained as we approached Morf's Modern Motors. 'It's already picked out and everything.'

'Let's go see it after work, Irene,' Leigh-Ann said. 'Let's go see the radio he's getting.' And laughing, she cupped her hands to her mouth and hollered in the direction of the garage, 'Let's have a look at the radio that *Big Lug Amel* is getting.'

There was no sign of Amel from the garage, only the hammering of an electric drill.

'Get it over with, Irene,' Leigh-Ann said. A logging truck passed us on the highway and we shielded our eyes and walked backwards into the dust. 'It's like when my horse Roger got the heaves from Hal Lawrence's bad hay. The worst is over when you can force yourself to look straight at it without blinking once.'

* * *

Leigh-Ann was a ward-aide in Emergency and Admitting where she helped admit babies with diarrhoea, women giving birth, men who'd broken a leg or chopped off a finger.

I worked in the Sterilizing Room where, mostly, I sharpened needles. Sometimes I was asked to help in packaging hot sterilized instruments in squares of cloth that we taped shut, then sterilized again. But the needles took most of my time.

My job was to collect the used needles from various parts of the hospital, then to clean them, first washing them, soaking them in rubbing alcohol, then going through them, one by one, sharpening each one on an electric grindstone.

I had to hold each needle at a certain angle, moving each one carefully into the turning grindstone, then check every one by pushing it through a gauze bandage. If the needle snagged, I had to sharpen it again, until it was perfectly angled, sharp and smooth.

When I closed my eyes at night, or even blinked too long in the daytime, I saw needles – needles in storage cylinders, needles in kidney basins, needles on the stainless steel counter, needles on the utility cart.

* * *

'Oh, I can't believe it,' Leigh-Ann said when we stood in front of the radio in the jewellery store window. 'It's so beautiful.'

I still had the ragged whine of the electric grindstone sounding in my ears. But when I forced myself to look at the radio, I could see what Leigh-Ann meant.

The cabinet of the radio was made of a caramel-coloured wood that had been curved down on one side, and around on the other. The opening for the sound wasn't one square as I would have expected, but several small openings placed in a pattern that resembled a church window.

The dial was round, and as large as my outspread hand. Radiating in concentric circles from the centre of the dial, there were numbers and the names of cities – Moscow, Madrid, London, Tokyo, Berlin. I remembered in school being told of a device sailors had used to navigate by the stars, and it seemed to me that the instrument they used must have resembled this dial.

'Well,' I said finally, stepping back from the window. 'I warned you.'

Side by side, we walked back along the sidewalk.

'Look at the bright side, Irene,' Leigh-Ann said. 'At least you get to see it. At least you get to have it in the house.'

Something like an invisible x-ray apron settled over me and weighed me down. I didn't answer her.

We were approaching the place where the Old Elks' Hall had burned down last year, and where a small new hall had risen in its place. There was a sign at the front made from a single sheet of plywood cut into the shape of an open book.

Leigh-Ann stopped and read the sign aloud in a syrupy, mock-religious voice. 'Are you friendless and alone? Have you lost your way? Let Jesus be your friend. Let Jesus show you the way. MIRACLE SERVICES, Pastor: Orville Watt.'

Usually I was the first to laugh at her jokes, but this time I just kept walking.

'You wouldn't catch me dead in there,' Leigh-Ann announced.

Without answering, I made a sharp right, walked up the dirt path and up the wooden steps. I glanced once at Leigh-Ann, then pulled open the pre-fab door.

'Irene!' Leigh-Ann called, her voice hushed but urgent, as if I was embarrassing her. 'I-*rene*!'

Inside, the hall was crowded with benches and people. Someone shook my hand and showed me to the front where I wedged myself down between a fat lady in a print housedress and another woman I'd seen working as a teller at the Royal Bank.

Then Leigh-Ann was there, trying to find a way to sit down beside me, but someone showed her to an empty spot nearer the back, and on the aisle.

I looked around at the walls of still unplastered Gyprock. The air smelled of people's bodies, stale perfume, wood and nails.

I looked over my shoulder at Leigh-Ann. She had the mournful look of someone trying not to laugh, but when she saw me, she clamped her hand over her mouth, her shoulders shaking, and jabbed her finger at the door.

I couldn't help laughing back.

But Mrs Vernon Rottwetter was already playing the electric organ, and a bear-shaped man in a baggy black suit – I guessed this was Orville Watt – was walking to the front where he proceeded to read something from the Bible, and to pray, his arms up, as if nailed to the air above his head.

When he brought his black bear arms down, it was silent for a full half-minute. Then Orville Watt spoke.

'There's nothing special about me,' he said, bringing his fierce dark eyes up to look at us. He spoke in a low voice, so quiet I had to stay motionless to hear him.

'I'm not so different from a lot of other men. A man in a coffee shop. A man in a bar. Behind the wheel of a gravel truck. Maybe working on a story about why the gravel's three days late. Maybe driving to see a woman who's not his woman. Maybe numbed against the pain of his life with liquor. I'm a brother to that man. I been in his shoes. I seen that place. I won't hide that from you.'

A trapped bee buzzed against the window.

'I have only one thing to my credit,' Orville Watt said, and he began to speak more forcefully. 'I opened my heart and let Jesus Christ into my life and was saved by the power of his grace and healed by his love.

'But let no man boast, sayeth the Lord. What I took, it was given freely unto me. It was a gift. It cost me nothing.

'All I did,' he said, shouting now, 'was to allow Jesus to bring the healing power of *his love* into *my life!* I opened the door of my heart – I said, Jesus, come in! – and Jesus did the rest!

'Are *you* ready to do that?' he asked, still shouting, watching us from his bear-snout face. 'Are you ready to let Jesus into your life?'

On the other side, a baby fussed and settled.

'Raise your hand if you're willing this evening – this moment – to let Jesus into your life.' He held his own square hand up, and scanned the rows with his small dark eyes.

I shifted my gaze to avoid his.

One by one, hands went up, slowly at first, then more and more of them. Voices called out, 'Yes!' or, 'I love you, Jesus!' I glanced back at Leigh-Ann, but she was sitting up straight, her hands folded on her lap, her eyes at the front, as if we'd gotten into trouble in school.

Orville Watt walked down the side and centre aisles. 'Praise Jesus, thank you, Jesus,' he said as he touched raised hands or the tops of heads. Someone behind me called out, then I felt the bank teller next to me raise her arm.

Orville Watt touched her hand and I heard his voice above me.

'Sometimes life is hard. Sometimes you feel alone. Sometimes you shut the door of your heart against life and against Jesus.'

As he spoke, I could see the door of my own heart. It was about a foot square, and made of thick, worn planks bolted together.

'Open your heart,' I heard Orville Watt say. 'Unlatch the door. Invite Jesus to shine in his holy redeeming light.'

I thought of that square door, allowed it to creak open a little, and instantly, I felt a deep warming light in the centre of my chest. Orville Watt touched the crown of my head and the light in my heart rippled out to the top of my head, where his hand was, to the tips of my fingers and the bones of my feet.

'Yes,' I said, and put up my hand.

'Praise be to Jesus,' Orville called. 'Hallelujah!' And he laid his hand on the back of my neck.

Then he was at the side again. Someone called out to him and he placed his hand on her head, and reached the other one up to pray.

I was no longer paying close attention to exactly what was happening to anyone else. Something had happened to me. I had become weightless, clear as glass, filled with light. I was transformed.

I was bright like a river. Not the river in town which was frozen over for half the year and brown with the sawmill for the other half. Not like the pastoral river we had on a calendar at home. This river was a living river in my own mind, a place that had always been there, but which I'd lost my way to, until now.

* * *

I was a little breathless when I got to Morf's Modern Motors, but everything inside me was connected. I was like a flashlight with high-powered batteries, positive connected to negative, and negative to positive. I could hardly wait for Amel to slide himself out from under the car he was working on.

'I *want* you to have that short-wave radio,' I said to Amel who was still on his back on the concrete floor. 'You're my brother, Amel. I love you and I *want* you to have that radio.'

Amel stood up, pulled a kerosene rag from the can on the counter, looked up at me, then down at his hands as he cleaned them.

'Have a Coke,' he said after a while, and scanned the counter for the opener. He took his time getting the Coke from the cooler, then opened one for himself and one for me.

'Ask me something, Irene,' he said, handing me the cold wet bottle. The Coke sparked and fizzed. 'Ask me do I want a short-wave radio.'

'What?' I said. 'What do you mean?'

'Ask me do I care about those provincial exams. Ask me do I feel cut out for school. Ask me do I want to be a druggist. Ask me what I want out of life. Go ahead,' he said as if challenging me to hit him. 'Go ahead. Ask.'

'I don't know,' I said. 'OK, what do you want?'

'You're like a whole lot of other people, Irene,' he said, looking out the rolled-up garage door with a wounded look. 'You know all about me, but you don't take the time to ask.'

The air hose lay in the doorway, hissing lightly.

'I'm not going back to school, Irene. I had a talk with Morf and I'm staying here. Pass or fail, it doesn't stack up a whole lot different to me.'

A day ago, an hour ago, I might have counselled Amel to think twice, to consider the future, to look before he leaped. I might have reminded him of our parents who hadn't had a chance to go to school. But now, I simply took in what he had to say.

Why not, I thought, why not. If Jesus was a man today, he might very well be working in this exact garage. He might be overhauling driveshafts, replacing ball-bearings, staring into transmissions, the same as Amel. And I pictured Jesus, a big man in oily overalls, a monkey wrench in his back pocket, whistling to himself, turning the lever to raise a car on the hydraulic lift.

I walked to the upended Coke crate. As I replaced my bottle, I noticed a lovely yellow light catching on it, and on the other empties. I stopped to look. As I watched, the light intensified to a brilliant liquid gold, then slowly spread to the red Coke cooler, to the work bench, to the tools, to the boxes of parts lined up on the shelves, to the floor and walls, until the entire garage was illuminated with an intense golden light.

Outside, the sun was low, but it shone brighter in the garage, like a radio at night, or a store window, like the original Christmas scene.

'Look,' I whispered to Amel. 'Do you see this?'

'What?' Amel said, squinting around at the walls.

'Do you see the light?' I asked. 'This garage is filled with golden light. Can you see it?'

Amel looked up at the rafters then back at me.

'Jesus is here, Amel,' I said. 'Why not choose this place? This garage is a holy place.'

'Cripes, Irene,' Amel said, lowering his voice. 'Cripes, get a handle on it.' He pulled on his welding mask, lowered the visor, then picked up a blow torch. 'You got to do something, Irene. You got to get yourself a boyfriend.'

* * *

When Orville Watt called out for testimonials, I was the first to stand. In school, our once-a-year five-minute public speech was an agony for me, but this wasn't like a speech. This was just me talking, and others listening.

'I spoke to my brother,' I said, and the electric organ music continued, but very softly now. 'I spoke to my brother with love, and a wonderful thing happened. A miracle happened. My brother, who was a stranger, isn't a stranger any longer. I know that someday, my brother will be my friend.'

Someone called out, 'Praise Jesus!' Orville Watt raised his clenched hands in the air with thanks, and even the electric organ music grew louder, before it became quiet again.

'I had a vision when I was in Morf's Modern Motors,' I continued. 'I was thinking about Jesus working the hydraulic lift, and suddenly the whole garage filled up with a kind of golden light.'

'This is the power of Jesus!' Orville called out. 'This is the miraculous healing power of love at work in the world today!'

'There was golden light everywhere,' I said, crying now, remembering the glory of it. 'On the Coke machine, on the oil drum, on all the tools and parts. Everything was flooded with gold. I could feel the presence of Jesus there.'

Someone called out, 'Hallelujah!' Orville Watt squeezed my shoulder and I could feel the cells of my body align like iron filings near a magnet.

I looked up and saw Leigh-Ann was there, and she was crying too. Mrs Vernon Rottwetter played the electric organ louder now, someone started to sing, and Orville Watt held up both hands like lightning rods and tears of joy ran down his face.

I felt like Madame Curie with her incredible, shining rock. I felt anointed. I felt I could shine in the dark.

I sat down again, trembling, but everything inside me completely connected. In my mind, I trained the power of love on

Leigh-Ann, forgiving her for her failures of friendship, for being so off-kilter where Amel was concerned. I shone the same light on my grade eight teacher who I saw on the other side of the hall. I shone it on Erma McNatty on the next bench who'd locked the doors of the dairy exactly at six o'clock, even though she saw me coming up the steps. I used it on the boards in the floor, on the nails in the Gyprock, on a refrigerated truck I saw passing the window.

I knew I wanted – maybe, I thought, I was called – to use this same light on the needles at work, so that they were no longer simple slivers of stainless steel, but more, until they hummed with order and purpose, like every other thing in God's creation.

* * *

'What are you telling everyone about Morf's Modern Motors?' Amel said at home. 'Why are you going around saying you saw Jesus working the hydraulic lift? I was there and there was no one else but me and you.'

'The hydraulic lift?' my mother said, looking up at me and almost burning herself with the coffee she was pouring into my dad's thermos. 'Who was working the hydraulic lift?'

I turned to my mother and father.

'There's something I have to tell you,' I said.

My dad reached for his thermos and got quickly to his feet, but my mother jerked on his sleeve and he sat down again. They each huddled in their own place and looked over at me.

I shut my eyes to tune in to the golden light inside me. This was harder than the time I spoke to Amel, but after a few moments, I opened my eyes and went ahead anyway.

'I forgive you,' I said. 'I have let the light of Jesus Christ shine into my heart, and have found it within myself to forgive you.'

My dad looked around the table as if checking for something he'd misplaced.

'I always thought you were my parents,' I said,

understanding this myself for the first time as I spoke. 'But you're not my parents.'

I looked at my mother. 'You're not my mother. You're my sister. And you're not really my father,' I said to my father, you're my brother. We're all children of God.

'Why shouldn't you give Amel a short-wave radio?' I continued. 'I don't begrudge Amel a short-wave radio. Even though you didn't get me a short-wave radio. Even though Amel doesn't even care if he gets a short-wave radio.'

'Don't talk crazy,' my dad said sternly, but glanced over to my mother with a frightened look.

'Why don't you go to the United Church, instead of to those Holy Rollers, if you want to go to church so bad,' my mother said. 'Sing in the United Church choir. Teach United Church Sunday school. I won't complain.'

'They got some kind of teen dances down there,' Amel said. 'Maybe you can hook up with some boy with ideas along the same lines as yourself.'

I thought of the dial on the short-wave radio with its concentric circles and numbers radiating from the centre, of the needle that could sweep around to any number on the dial. In a single power surge that seemed to electrify the circuits of my brain, I suddenly understood about different churches, different religions, maybe, I thought, about life itself.

'It's like the numbers on a radio dial,' I said, fumbling for words to explain. I put my forefinger down on the table and swung my thumb around to show them. 'You see! Everything's connected! God is everywhere!'

After a few moments my mother spoke.

'Maybe you should have bought her a short-wave radio,' she said to my dad. 'Maybe we should order her one of those matching suitcase sets for when she leaves home.'

The golden river inside me grew very still, seized, then reared up in a kind of tidal wave.

I jumped up, smashing my elbow into an open cupboard

door behind me, but noticing in the back of my mind that I felt no pain.

'I don't want your short-wave radio!' I yelled. 'I passed grade ten last year! That was your chance to buy me a short-wave radio! I don't want a matching suitcase set! You're too late! You're way too late!'

* * *

'What are you doing here?' I asked Amel, who sat on a chair in Emergency and Admitting.

Amel was pumping a black rubber bulb attached to a band around his arm, apparently taking his own blood pressure. A ward-aide I didn't know was collapsed in a chair beside him, laughing a tinkling laugh.

'What's wrong?' I said, my hands on the handle of the stainless steel utility cart. 'Where's Leigh-Ann?'

I was making my end-of-shift rounds, delivering clean needles to the various wards, and collecting the used ones. I always stopped a while in Emergency and Admitting to visit with Leigh-Ann. It didn't seem like her to neglect this opportunity to check Amel's vital signs.

'So hello to you, too,' Amel said in his handsome, wounded way. 'Not too much wrong with me, about Leigh-Ann I couldn't say, but Jack there, he should see a doctor.'

In the shadows behind the moveable curtain, I could see Jack-the-Jeweller sitting on the side of a stretcher, holding a blue plastic ice-pack to his eyebrow.

'You can't cancel a special order,' Jack croaked at me. 'You can't special-order a short-wave radio, then up and cancel when the wind shifts.' He glowered balefully at me with his one good eye from where he sat on the stretcher.

Amel pinched the bridge of his nose and shook his head. The ward-aide tinkled.

'The doctor will be with you shortly, sir,' she called out from where she sat.

'So the exam results come in and Dad hauls off and ploughs Jack-the-Jeweller there,' Amel explained into my ear. 'Jack comes to the house a-hollering he's taking the old man to court, so the old man up and hits him.'

My sterile paper cap crinkled.

'The results are in?' I said. 'Did you pass?'

'Too much religion,' Amel explained to the ward-aide. 'Hello. Hello. Irene.'

He passed his hand once, then twice, before my eyes.

I noticed Jack-the-Jeweller turn his blue plastic ice-pack over, then put it back to his eye.

'One, the results come in,' Amel said, speaking extra loudly and clearly, with an eye to entertaining the ward-aide. 'Two, Dad cancels the special order. Three, Jack hits the roof. Four, Dad hits Jack. Five, the cops pull up, sirens a-wailing, lights a-flashing, and take Dad in.'

The information whirled in front of me with the speed of an electric grindstone.

'Jack, he's left a-sitting with his swole-up eye and his hang-dog look, so number next, I eat my sandwich, and I drive Jack in.'

'The short-wave radio?' I asked. 'What happened to the short-wave radio?'

'My sister, Irene, wishes to inquire about the short-wave radio,' Amel said, nodding to himself with a show of manly patience. 'Listen to me, Irene. Try to understand. Go down to the hardware store, go in through the front door, and go straight to Mrs Guy Staniski behind the cash. Say, ''Mrs Guy Staniski, I wish to purchase a radio.'' Say it loud and clear, Irene. It's going to run you, probably, fifteen dollars.'

* * *

Through the black bars of the jail cell, I saw my dad lying flat on his back on a high, narrow cot. His hands were folded on his chest, and he was staring up at the freshly painted green ceiling. He looked small and old.

I thought several things. Someday, my dad would die. When he was a boy, he'd wanted to go to school. And no one else I knew had a family that was so much trouble as mine.

Beside me, my mother sat rocking herself on a metal folding chair, her face in a piece of Kleenex.

When she looked up at me, I saw she was laughing.

'Partridge soup,' she wheezed, tears welling up in her eyes, 'He thinks they gave him partridge soup!' She patted her hands on her lap, laughing silently up at me, as if expecting me to find this funny too.

'Can you picture it?' she whispered. 'Can you picture the Mounties hunting the partridge down? Plucking out the feathers? Partridge! I'll bet you it was chicken noodle!'

There was the sound of voices, then two Mounties clipped down the stairs. We saw their black shoes first, then the yellow stripe down the side of their pants, then their faces.

One of them snapped a ring-binder open and shut, then rapidly read out a list of numbers and phrases, section-this, and sub-section-that. None of it would stick in my brain long enough for me to make sense of it.

'In a case like this,' the other one said, 'we generally hold them a couple hours to let things simmer down.'

I left my mother standing on the front steps of the RCMP detachment. I wanted to put as much distance as I could, and as quickly as possible, between myself and my luckless family.

I hurried two blocks over to Orville Watt's Meeting Hall.

I was an hour early for the evening service, but the door was unlocked as usual, and I went in and sat down on a bench near the front.

I wanted to hear the word of God tonight. I wanted to sing and pray. I wanted to testify. I wanted Orville Watt to call out, to shake, to hold up his arms, to lay his hands on me.

I heard the door open, and turned around.

It was Leigh-Ann, not in her ward-aide uniform, but in her star-spangled cowgirl dress that she wore for the Stampede.

Just behind her, almost shadowing her, was Orville Watt. When they saw me, they stopped and smiled, both of them smiling in the same shy, shiny way.

Leigh-Ann flicked her pony tail against Orville's shoulder, and Orville brought his open hand to the side of her beaded cowgirl belt, not quite touching it.

I remembered I was still wearing my hospital uniform, and scuffed white hospital oxfords.

'Leigh-Ann and I were planning on drawing up the the roster for the Welcome Committee,' Orville said, stepping out from behind her. 'We'd be happy if you could help us, Irene.'

It seemed to me I could smell needles from my yellow hospital uniform. I thought of the needles, how cold they were, how sharp, how numerous, and suddenly I knew I was very tired and had to go home and lie down.

'I don't think so,' I said. 'I don't think I can help with the roster for the Welcome Committee.'

I stood up from the bench, walked past them, out the door, and down to the sidewalk.

It was evening now, and still light. It seemed to take many times the normal number of steps to get home.

The air along the highway hurt my throat. Everything, the stores, the trees, the pick-up trucks, were layered with a fine film of dust. I remembered hearing that the town council had promised to oil the highway against dust, and it seemed to me now that this was long overdue.

When I passed Morf's Modern Motors, I looked up. Morf's Modern Motors was really no more than a two-bit sort of place, I saw with surprise. It was no more than four walls and a roof thrown up against wind and rain.

I remembered the incredible golden light and it seemed to me unlikely that such a thing could have ever really happened there. It must have been my imagination. Maybe the setting sun had slanted in at an unusual angle that day. Maybe there'd been sun spots. Maybe light had refracted off the metal and glass to create such an effect. There must have been, I thought, an everyday explanation I'd overlooked at the time.

I realized then that I'd lost it – the connectedness, the order, the radiance, that different way of seeing. I'd hooked into a different wave-length, then suddenly I'd lost the frequency.

When I got home, I walked past my mother who was crying noisily at the kitchen table.

'I've got to lie down,' I said. 'I'm coming down with something.' I went to my room, lay down on the bed, and pulled the sheets over my head.

If only, I thought, if only.

But these sheets were just sheets. My hospital uniform was just a smelly old hospital uniform. My mother crying in the kitchen was just my mother crying, nothing unusual in that.

And Orville Watt? What of him? Why wouldn't he fit into the dusty broom closet along with everything else? Why wouldn't he shrink back into the colourless, the drab, the ordinary?

It would help if I could see Orville Watt as just another half-baked Holy Roller, but I couldn't.

I hobbled to the kitchen to gargle with salt water and back to my bedroom to tie a dirty sock around my throat. Salt water and a dirty sock was usually a reliable cure for a sore throat.

But this time it didn't work.

Maps of the Known World

WHEN I WAS SIXTEEN, my father brought home a man for me to marry. The man's name was Pete Paska and he sat down at the kitchen table without needing to be asked twice.

I was at the other end of the table, chewing the flavour out of a pack of gum, two or three sticks at a time, my history book open to a chapter called 'The Glory that was Greece'.

'Such a man! Such a man!' my father said, grinning at my mother and me, but mostly at Pete Paska. 'He can speak perfect English and perfect Ukrainian. Who's going to make Irene a better husband than this?'

I stopped chewing when I heard my name.

My father's face was flushed and happy, and Pete Paska's face was a shiny birthday balloon. They brought the smell of snow and whisky into the house with them.

'He's got a good indoor job down there at the train station,' my father said, pressing Pete Paska's shoulder. 'He's a man for the future! He's a man for progress! He's a man for action!'

'See this salt-shaker?' Pete Paska asked loudly, pointing at the rabbit-shaped salt-shaker in the middle of the table. He had a forceful manner and I couldn't help but pay attention.

'Is this salt-shaker going to move by itself?' he demanded. He looked around at us, but didn't wait for anyone to answer. 'No! It will not!' he said. 'It moves when someone moves it!' Then he picked up the salt-shaker and held it dramatically over the table, giving us a minute to take this in.

My father grinned happily.

Irene. Man. Husband. Future. I heard every word my father said.

I stared at Pete Paska from behind my bangs. I'd never seen him closer than across the street, or connected him with anything except, in a general sort of way, the train station.

He was an older man. Twenty-six or twenty-seven, maybe. He was shorter than my father, but more muscular. He had dark eyes, wavy black hair, and slightly yellowish, gnawed-down looking teeth, the kind some small industrious animal might have, a beaver, say, or a muskrat. I got a good view of his teeth because he smiled at me every few minutes.

I looked up for a while, but then tried to go back to my homework. We were having a test and our teacher was known to ask trick questions, such as what was the name of Alexander-the-Great's horse.

'She's shy,' my father said, as he placed two whisky glasses on the table, one in front of Pete Paska and one in front of himself.

'Still water runs deep,' Pete Paska said, and smiled at me again.

My mother, her back a brick wall, kept washing dishes. She banged cups onto the shelf, clattered forks into the drawer, and slammed pots into the cupboard.

'*Di Bozheh!*' my father said, toasting Pete Paska. 'To your health!' He held up his glass which had a donkey painted on it.

'*Di Bozheh!*' Pete Paska answered. His glass had a rooster on it.

'To the Old Country!'

'To the New Country!'

'To Family!'

'To Marriage!'

'To Progress!'

'To the Future!'

'To Action!'

'Why are you in all of a sudden such a hurry to marry her off?' my mother yelled the second Pete Paska shut the door behind him. 'What's the big rush? She's got lots of time yet to get married!'

'He counts for something in this town,' my father said, still happy from the good time he'd had with Pete Paska. 'He's a Big Wheel down there at the train station. Four guys working for him and it's all the time, "Yes, Pete! No, Pete! Anything you say, Pete!".'

'What about school?' my mother countered. 'Shouldn't she at least finish school? Shouldn't she finish school and work for a while like the other girls?'

'You think men like Pete Paska grow like mushrooms after the rain?'

My mother swept the floor and scooped the dust into the wood stove which sat alongside the newer gas range.

'At least let her finish the year,' she said, clinking the round lid back onto the wood stove. 'At least let her finish grade eleven.'

I heard the bedsprings creak in my parents' bedroom off the kitchen. I knew my father was sitting down to take his shoes off.

'You think she's better off with one of those Jailbird-Johannsens?' he called out. 'Or maybe that shiftless Bert Strain? People like you, they never know when they got it good.' The bedsprings creaked again. 'Perfect English! And perfect Ukrainian!'

As I rested my head and arms on the table, I noticed I hardly breathed. I hardly had to. This wasn't new, though. Sometimes I could go for long periods, hardly breathing at all. At school we learned about evolution and how fish climbed out of the ocean and developed lungs. Something like that was happening to me too, I thought, though in my case it was going one step further. In my case, it felt as though I was gradually getting to the point where I didn't need to breathe at all. It didn't seem strange though, no more so than other things that happened, growing pains in my legs, or cramps before my period.

When I went to bed, I found I could hardly shut my eyes. There were two places. This place, this shadowy, half-secret, hard-to-breathe-in world of home, and the other place, the fast-paced, too-bright world of school, homework, tests, who-said-what, who-likes-who, the Valentine's Dance.

I flipped my pillow over and ran through the times tables which had always put me to sleep before. In the distance I could hear the trains – Pete Paska's trains – call out to one another. I imagined them racing past the things we'd drawn on maps at school – black pencil-crayoned oil derricks, golden sheaves of wheat, apple orchards, smoky factories, cities whose names we'd had to copy from the atlas, and fish emblazoned on the blue and wavy sea.

* * *

The next morning, when I went to the kitchen, my mother was stirring the porridge and crying.

'When I got married,' she said, 'I thought, poor man, he needs a woman to cook and clean for him. I thought washing his clothes was all I had to do.' She blew her nose and turned, embarrassed but stubborn, to look at me. 'There's more to it than that, though. A man expects more. Did you know that?'

A mouthful of scalding tea stopped at the top of my throat. I stood up, managed to swallow, then placed my cup on the table. My mother followed me as I got my homework, zipped it into my binder, put on my parka and boots.

'You know about that, don't you?' she asked as I opened the door to leave. 'You know what happens, don't you?'

I rushed out into the stinging cold, my cheeks burning, my plastic binder stiff in my hands. I put my head down into the wind and walked as fast as I could toward the school.

Terrible things could happen, I knew that. Take your average awful thing, multiply by four, and that was probably closer to the truth. Your car could get cut in two on the railroad tracks. You could get put in an iron lung. You could have your leg eaten off by a bear, like the new Pentecostal minister. Barely believable things happened between men and women in bed – somehow I wasn't totally surprised – then after those things there was the business of childbirth, of being strapped to a delivery table, of screaming in pain, of possibly bleeding to death, see, I knew about that.

And what was that other terrible thing hovering behind me like a black dog just outside my field of vision? I stopped walking for a moment to let it take shape in my mind, and then rushed on. Oh yes, you could have Pete Paska, smiling and muskrat-toothed, waiting to marry you.

* * *

At school, we talked about the Valentine's Dance. Everyone was on a committee. I'd signed up for the decorating committee in a smaller sub-committee charged with the responsibility of making three hundred pink Kleenex flowers for the huge heart on stage.

Beverly Cox, Gwen Farris, Stacey Reed and I sat in a circle of chairs in the over-heated typing room with ten boxes of pink Kleenex, and talked about who was going with who to the dance. Beverly and Stacey had definitely been asked, Gwen had sort of been asked, and I was pretty sure I was about to be asked. Bryce Bliss had turned around in math class to help me with my math for two days in a row, and I thought it highly possible that he would ask me. As far as I knew, he hadn't asked anyone else.

None of the four of us had new dresses for the dance, but as we pleated and fluffed the pink Kleenex, we agreed unanimously that new clothes were not what counted. What counted was a girl's personality. After all, it wasn't as if this was our wedding day. For our weddings, naturally we planned to go whole hog.

For our weddings we would have to choose between taffeta, satin, *peau de soie* and white velvet. We would be forced to consider whether our veils would be cocktail length, chapel length, or ankle length. Would our necklines be high or low?

Would our sleeves be lily-pointed or short and worn with long white gloves?

Gwen told us that the red-haired girl at the telephone office had just married, not in a wedding gown, but in an ordinary good dress. 'It makes sense,' Gwen pointed out. 'Why not buy a dress you'll be able to wear again and again?'

Although the talk of wedding gowns made me nervous, I voted against economizing in this way.

'After all,' I pointed out, 'a girl needs something to look forward to besides just doing the man's laundry and so forth.'

'Irene always makes sex sound so awful,' Stacey Reed said with a superior smile. 'I don't think sex is awful. I think sex is beautiful, like a painting of a sunset, or classical music.'

Classical? I thought with alarm. *Classical?* I liked Hawaiian better.

'No worse than a hog through a chute,' said Beverly Cox, who lived on a farm.

'Horses do it,' someone said. 'Cows. Pigs.'

'Earthworms.'

'No, stupid,' the others said.

I dumped the Kleenex flowers on the floor. 'What number are we up to?' I asked. 'I better count them.'

'What's wrong, Irene?' Stacey laughed. 'You look ready to faint. You're afraid of all that, aren't you? I bet you are. I bet you're scared stiff of your wedding night.'

'Yes,' I said, losing count. 'I mean, no.' The girls laughed again.

We glued the Kleenex flowers onto a huge heart-shaped sheet of cardboard we'd pieced together from boxes.

On the intercom, the principal said that the Valentine's Dance was in grave danger of being cancelled if students failed to apply themselves more diligently to the curriculum as laid out by the ministry.

At the end of the day, the grade eleven students were called back to the history room because of the poor results of the history test. Apparently some answers had been scrawled indifferently in pencil. Other papers had been handed in under false names. Jokes had been offered in response to the essay question: Describe the principle that Archimedes discovered in his bath.

The class was given a penalty assignment which was to be copied from the board. The teacher, however, made an exception for five students who had, he said, approached the test in a suitably serious manner. The list was read aloud and I was one of them.

As the five of us picked up our books and left the room, Bryce Bliss – the boy I'd hoped would ask me to the dance – looked up with blanket contempt, and called after us, 'Hens!'

* * *

At home I ground graham crackers, corn syrup and condensed milk into a mash and ate it from the mixing bowl. Then I went to my bedroom and lay down on the covers.

I woke when my mother pushed open my bedroom door.

'He's here,' she said. 'He wants to see you.' It was dark and the light from the kitchen shone behind her so I couldn't see her face.

'Who's here?'

'Pete Paska.'

'Pete Paska? What does he want *me* for?'

My mother looked back toward the kitchen and rubbed her fingertips on the bib of her apron.

'Tell him I'm in bed.'

'In bed? But it's only seven.'

'Tell him I'm not here.'

'How am I supposed to say that?' she hissed. 'He knows you're here. Just talk to him. It's not going to kill you just to talk to him.'

I felt my forehead for fever, then finally stood up and went to the kitchen. I felt like I'd eaten a tin can.

Pete Paska was spreading income tax forms and an open ledger on the table. He stepped back to check the all-over effect, then looked up at me and smiled.

'A thief hides a crust of bread, but an honest man hides nothing!' he said. 'Come. Let's get your dad.'

My mother frowned and rubbed her hand on her forehead, but handed me my parka and boots.

Pete Paska's car, still idling at the front of the house, was hot and smelled of over-sweet perfume from the tree-shaped air-freshener that hung on the rearview mirror. He adjusted various dials, fans and mirrors. I sat with my shoulder pressed against the side door and tried to block the scent of the air-freshener by breathing as little as possible.

I expected to drive straight downtown to get my dad, but I could see Pete Paska was looping around the other way, taking the scenic route. We drove past Ed Ferleyko's Garage, past the Pearly Gates Motel, past the Ukrainian church, then approached the school where there were already lights on in readiness for the Valentine's Dance.

I breathed in a strangulated way because of the air-freshener. What was happening? Where was I headed? I was sixteen, but it seemed as if my life had already flown away from me and dissolved into the night. What lay ahead? Nothing but cooking and cleaning, plus the other things men expected in addition.

'Life is for the living,' Pete Paska observed energetically. I could feel the force of his smile through the hot perfumey air of the car.

'I have to throw up,' I said.

Pete Paska pulled over immediately.

I got out, grateful to be near the school, and ran to the boys' washroom on the main floor. But I couldn't relax with the tall white urinals looming up like tombstones behind me. And besides, now that I was away from the air-freshener, I felt better. I decided to go upstairs to the girls' washroom.

Upstairs, the lights were off, except for the typing room, where the huge Kleenex flower heart was still drying on the floor. Someone had left the window open and snow had blown in on one side of the heart. I tried to dust the snow off, but some of it had already melted, and the heart was soggy on one side.

I pulled the cushioned teacher's chair over to the open window, and leaned back, letting the blowing snow melt on my face. I reached onto the roof that extended below the window and made several small snowballs which I ate slowly, one at a time.

On the window ledge, there was a textbook someone had left open to a picture. *Ptolemy draws a map of the known world*, the caption said.

The picture showed a handsome man in bathrobe-type clothes. He was drawing at a table, while four other men looked on, admiring.

When I look at the picture, I felt a dull weight behind my eyes. How could this man be so public? So sure of himself? Would it really be so easy for him? Wouldn't there be people who said, 'Don't do that – be careful – you've got it wrong?'

I was still trying to figure this out when I heard heavy footsteps in the hall. I jumped up to move the chair back, but the person almost instantly appeared in the doorway.

It was Pete Paska.

'I've been waiting,' he said. His outline was as clear as if it'd been drawn with India ink. He was no longer smiling.

'This is getting wrecked here,' I said, pointing to the heart.

He didn't say anything.

'Could you do just one thing?' I said. 'Could you take it downstairs to the gym?'

'What good is this?' he said, and stared at me for a moment. 'This is for kids.' But he picked it up.

'Turn right at the bottom, then left,' I said, watching as he started to manoeuvre the slightly soggy heart downstairs. 'I'll just be a minute. Maybe two.'

I needed at least that long to kill myself.

There was stapler on the desk – too small, I thought. There was a large guillotine-style paper-cutter on the table – too big, I told myself. Then I looked at the open window and stepped out onto the roof. This was just right, I thought, and felt pleased with my own little joke.

I'd been here before, though never in winter. Sometimes in spring, I climbed out here with a few other girls to eat lunch and scratch our initials into the hot tar of the roof. One girl – Jeanette Tremblay – pulled off pieces of the tar which she chewed like gum, but I was never able to develop a taste for it.

I waded through the snow to the edge of the roof and looked down. It was further down than I remembered. There were two tar barrels directly below where I was, so I moved along the edge of the roof until there was nothing but the flat snowy schoolyard beneath me.

There was the exact spot where we'd built a snow fort in grade five, boys against the girls, which had been so much simpler. There was the flagpole where Ollie Stout had frozen his tongue, just beyond, the road I walked to school every day. Nearby, I could see the shadows of the willows along the river where I swam in summer, worrying that my mother would kill me if I drowned.

The snowflakes were big and slow now. In the distance, I could make out my own house, with its tiny yellow kitchen window and snow blanketing the roof, as pretty from where I stood as a house on a Christmas card. In the other direction, I could even make out the dark shape of the hospital where I'd been born. I felt like a ghost looking out over my own life. I felt fine.

Behind me, the lights in the typing room went off, then on again.

'No one's here,' I heard someone say.

Then Pete Paska said my name.

I took a deep breath, a little run, and jumped.

There was a flash of light, but no sound. I folded silently like a Monopoly board. Then there was nothing.

After some time, I felt a burning pain in my arm and shoulder, but tried to ignore it. Snow started to melt and trickle down the back of my neck. I shifted my head, one arm, then the other.

Finally, I stood up and dusted myself off.

From where I stood, I could see Pete Paska's car still idling in front, the headlights catching on the falling snow. And beyond that, were two or three cars pulling into the parking lot at the far end of the yard.

I turned in the dark snowy playground, and walked the opposite way, in the direction of downtown. When I came to the lighted window of the laundromat, I opened the door and went in to warm up.

But it was different from the last time I was here. The rows of washing machines were gone. There were only orange chairs along one wall, and a canvas mailbag and cardboard boxes along the other side. Maxine Jack, with her dyed hair and her police dog, was behind the counter. Maxine Jack and her police dog meant this was the new bus depot. The police dog looked at me and rumbled, but stayed where it was.

I sat down on one of the orange vinyl chairs. The room still smelled of bleach and soap. On the wall there was a bus schedule that had been kissed here and there with lipsticked lips. I was shaky, and my left arm and shoulder still burned.

Beside me, someone lit a cigarette, then held the open pack out to me. He was a tall man in a black cowboy hat.

When I reached for a cigarette, I found my hand was shaking so much I had to steady it with my other one. My left arm hurt when I moved it, but I lifted it again to steady my wrist when the man lit my cigarette.

I pulled on the smoke, then breathed it out. My eyes watered and my lungs felt hot, but I was determined not to choke.

Outside, a car streaked past, travelling much too fast for the roads. I looked out, but only saw red tail lights receding into the storm.

I could feel the man in the black cowboy hat watching me.

'You always shake like that?' he asked.

I held out my almost fluttering hands, and watched them a moment, surprised by them myself.

'I'll get over it,' I said.

I pulled the smoke into my lungs and pushed it out. Pulled it in, pushed it out.

'Inhale,' I told myself. 'Exhale. Inhale, exhale.'

It was warm and, for the moment, peaceful here. I decided not to think about what I was going to do next.

I sat on the orange chair. I breathed in and out. I watched the cigarette smoke trail and twist toward the ceiling.

Influence of the Moon

'IT'S THE MOON that causes the tides in the ocean,' I told my father at the supper table. 'Everyone knows that.'

I centred my gold watch on my wrist, ate two forkfuls of sausages and potatoes, then pressed my hands hard against the prickly rollers that covered my head.

'See,' I said, trying to make this easy for my father to understand, 'what happens is, the moon pulls the water up.'

I was in high school this year and we were doing the periodic table and atomic weights. The moon and the tides were from back in grade eight. I watched my father but he only stared straight ahead, lifted his fork to his mouth, chewed and swallowed.

I glanced across to my mother and my brother Amel, adjusted one of the pink plastic pics that were stuck through my rollers, then looked back to my father.

'Tides on the ocean aren't just like waves on a lake,' I said. 'Tides are totally different.'

'Yap, yap, yap,' my dad said, finally looking at me in the blue-white fluorescent light of the kitchen. 'If you have nothing to say, it's better to keep quiet.'

Because we were at the supper table, my dad's dark green cap was politely pushed back, so it was loose on his head with the peak angled up. His almost white hair was pressed flat to his head, and the blue veins on his temples and hands stood out like rivers on a map. He looked over to my mother, but she was bending over her plate, eating quickly. She tugged at the collar of her dress to make room for the goitre which lay on the side of her neck, a doughy-looking swelling, as large as a fist.

'Well,' I said, looking over to Amel. 'What's true is true.'

Amel used to help me with these arguments. Not long ago, he would start them himself.

'Just think what a great invention the wheel is,' Amel would say, shaking his head in partly staged and partly real amazement. 'Don't you pity the poor jokers who had to do without it?'

'The wheel is easy,' our dad would answer. 'I could of invented the wheel.'

'It's easy for you because you've already seen the idea,' Amel would counter, dropping his jaw and rubbing his finger against his lip so as not to laugh.

'I would see a log,' our father would answer, stubbornly ignoring our knowing looks and grins. 'And I would think, why not cut it cross-ways and run something through the middle?'

This time, in the matter of the moon and the tides, Amel glanced over at me, but kept shaking the salt over his food. When he put the salt down, he started on the pepper.

'The moon!' our father said, tossing the words down like a two-bit bet on a poolroom table. 'You're talking crazy!'

* * *

Every day at six-thirty, my father came home from his job at the poolroom for supper. Afterwards, he put his parka and boots back on, and went back for the evening when business was best.

Close to midnight, he would clear out the customers, lock the doors, turn out the lights, and hide his money. Sweeping the floors and emptying the spittoons was left for Sundays.

'What if he has a heart attack or someone hits him over the head one night?' our mother said to Amel. 'Get him to tell me or you where he hides his money.'

'The Old Man does OK,' Amel answered her. 'Four break-ins but no one could find the cash.'

That was true. Even the Johannsen twins, who'd done three

months for it, had only been able to take cigarettes, dimes from the Coke machine, and a cigar box of watches and rings that had been pawned to my father in the poolroom.

The Johannsen twins would have stolen the gold watch I was now wearing, except that, two days before the break-in, my dad'd decided that the man who'd pawned it was not returning for it, so my dad gave the watch to me.

The watch was large for a lady's watch, and heavy. It had a flexible band made of gold, leaf-shaped segments accordioned together. The face of the watch, which was also gold, was decorated with two real diamonds, one at three o'clock, and one at nine.

'The diamonds must be real,' my mother had pointed out. 'Why else would they be so small?' The diamonds were tiny points of almost invisible light. They were so small they were almost hidden by the claws that held them. They were so small it made me feel cross-eyed to look at them.

'The moon's influence on the tides has been scientifically proven,' I said. 'It's been proven for ages.'

My father's lips moved soundlessly for a moment. 'It's no use to prove it,' he finally said, 'if it's not true.'

* * *

My mother reached across the table for a slice of bread, then turned her head and again pulled at the collar of her brown wool dress. Her face was pale with face powder and she was wearing her good dress because it was Tuesday, and on Tuesdays and Thursdays she still went to Prayer Meetings with the two tall thin ladies who'd come to town.

The two tall thin ladies, believed to be sisters, were called Miss Pym and Miss Pym, even by each other.

Miss Pym and Miss Pym lived in a rented room above the Royal Bank, wore their grey hair in matching grey nets, and held Prayer Meetings in people's houses.

For over two weeks now I'd gone to Prayer Meetings with

my mother, but now I wouldn't go anymore.

When I quit, my mother wept, saying she was begging on bended knee for me to go to meetings with her.

This was not actually true, I noticed. My mother's knees weren't bent at all. In fact, my mother stood with both feet solidly on the kitchen linoleum. She ripped arm's-lengths of toilet paper from a roll she kept on top of the fridge, stopped crying long enough to blow her nose, then cried again.

'First she's so religious! Then she's not religious!' she accused, crying. 'Why do you take everything to extremes? Why do you go out of your way to be an oddball? Why?'

Now, at the supper table with the discussion of moon and tides, my mother lifted her round powdered face to look at my dad and me.

'Eat,' she said. 'Eat before your supper gets cold. Moon or no moon, what does it matter?'

* * *

'Anyone who asks, I tell them the same thing,' my mother said, easing herself down onto a chair across the kitchen table from me. 'I tell them I'm not going back to the doctor. No matter what.'

I was sitting over the hot-air vent, filling out an order from the catalogue for a turquoise Ban-Lon sweater with a spray of pearls decorating the right shoulder.

The hot air from the furnace ballooned out my skirt, almost roasting my legs. The sweater I was ordering was featured on the cover of the catalogue, which showed a blonde girl in the turquoise sweater looking into an arrangement of mirrors which reflected into each other so that the reflections of the girl went on forever.

'I'm not going back to the doctor,' my mother said again. 'Not even if he comes to the door and puts a gun to my head.'

My mother'd had an operation the year before to have her goitre taken out, but it had grown right back, this time even bigger than before. It pressed against her throat and her windpipe, even, it seemed, against her heart.

'The doctor needed to keep me awake for the operation,' my mother explained, rubbing the palms of her hands back and forth along the table. 'I could hear him swear. I could hear him throw his knives on the floor. I would never go back. Not for a hundred dollars. Not for two hundred.'

I felt a thin hot pain in my own throat, as if a knife was cutting in.

'That orange-haired Olga Olanski from the drugstore said she had terrible headaches until she went to those Prayer Meetings with those two tall thin ladies. She says ten meetings, that's all it took. Boy, that's pretty easy!' She bent over the table and laughed to herself for a minute, then looked back at me. 'Just think if it was that easy!'

'Try it,' I said, my hands on my own throat. 'You try it.'

The catalogue slipped to the floor, where it fluttered until the furnace shut off a minute later.

'Who knows if it's the same thing this time? What if it's something worse?'

With the furnace shut off, I could feel the cold press in from every side, through the rags stuffed around the edges of the window, through the old coat that blocked the draught under the door.

'No doctor, no operation, no nothing,' my mother said. 'Could that happen?'

'Go.'

'I don't have the gall. I would stick out like a sore thumb.' My mother braced her hands on the table to stand, then moved to turn the propane on under the kettle. 'You go. You go, then maybe I'll come.'

* * *

Later, the night I heard the angels, I knew what they were right away.

Their voices were even, matter-of-fact, harmonious. I couldn't make out the words, but I often found that the case with choirs.

I did, however, recognize the tone.

They had the same worldly, uncompromising sound as certain girls in school – the ones who knew things – how to wear their boyfriends' jackets slung indifferently over their shoulders, how to draw pouts on their mouths with white lipstick, how to slouch down the halls with perfect nonchalance.

It sounded as though there were quite a few angels, a half-dozen or more, and it seemed to me that they were hovering in formation right outside the kitchen window. Because of the ice on the window, it was impossible to see them, but I didn't need to, I knew exactly what the angels looked like. I knew in that immediate inexplicable way I sometimes knew the phone was about to ring, or whether a particular toss of a coin would turn out heads or tails.

The angels had sleek feathery wings, expressionless faces, back-combed yellow hair, and they shone with their own light, like angels on Christmas cards, or like road signs in the dark. Sometimes one or two of them sang, sometimes all of them. The angels were perfect. They were amazing. And they were terrifying.

* * *

'When I shoot pool,' my father said to me across the salt and pepper shakers, the teapot, the pans of sausages, peas, and boiled potatoes, 'when I shoot pool, the guys will yell, "Do this! Do that!" Do I believe what any fool tells me?' He paused, still looking at me across the table, then answered himself. 'No! I see it for myself!' He pointed two fingers out like rays and beamed them slowly around the kitchen, at the potato peels on the counter, the poolroom calendar on the wall, the large white refrigerator crowded into the corner between the bathroom and the kitchen window.

This was our first fridge. Up to now, my mother had made

do with putting milk down the well in summer, or along windowsills in winter.

A driller from the oil rigs had pawned the fridge to my dad in the poolroom for thirty-five dollars, and when the man left town without reclaiming it, my dad took the fridge home for our own use.

Occasionally other things came to us in this way, a chrome statue of a bucking bronco, which was now on a bureau in the living room, a camera, and of course, watches. Amel and I had always had good watches to wear to school, though none had been as valuable or as good-looking as the gold one I had now.

'Forget the moon and let him eat,' my mother said to me as she poured my father a cup of tea. 'Can't you see he's getting blue in the face? What fun do you get out of torturing him like this?'

My father speared a sausage with his fork, cut it, and put a section in his mouth where its outline was still visible through his cheek. He washed it down with a mouthful of tea, leaned toward my mother and pretended to laugh.

'I say white, so she says black.' He laughed soundlessly again. 'What she wants, is everyone to notice her.'

I adjusted a pic from my rollers. 'How did they do that experiment about the tides?' I asked Amel. 'Is that the one where you swing a pail around in a circle?'

Amel buttered and neatly folded a slice of bread, then took a bite out of it.

'That would be centrifugal force,' he said.

Since Amel had decided he was through with school, and had got a job at Morf's Modern Motors, he was different with me. He no longer called me names, mirrored my movements to mix me up, or fought me for leg-room under the kitchen table. He became polite, which was the last thing I was prepared for, distant, a little edgy. At first, I would check myself to see if I had a rip, a smell, or blood on the back of my skirt.

He twanged his voice like a cowboy in a movie when he

greeted me at the supper table, or if we happened to meet in front of the Elite Café. 'Cold enough for ya?' he drawled. 'Steer clear of them wooden nickels!'

I spoke to Amel again. 'How does that experiment go then?'

'I don't know,' Amel said, stretching his hands to crack his knuckles. 'I don't remember one for the moon and the tides.' He thought for a minute, then shook his head. 'I can't see what kind of experiment they could rig up for that.'

* * *

'Don't mention the fridge,' my mother said into my ear the night it was our turn to have the Prayer Meeting at our house. 'They'll think we're bragging.'

My mother and I were still in the kitchen. My mother was stacking sandwiches on plates, but the ladies were already seated in an almost silent circle in the front room. Mrs Jack Hinkey, Mrs Pud Perry, and the orange-haired Olga Olanski weighed down the couch. The more-in-charge Miss Pym sat in the good chair, and the other Miss Pym sat on the stool from the sewing machine.

My mother's hair was ferociously bobby-pinned back and beads of sweat were already showing through her face powder, under her eyes and on her upper lip.

She'd spent the day dusting, polishing, ironing, making a marble cake and two kinds of sandwiches, chopped egg and mock-chicken. Halfway through the afternoon, she'd burned a hole in the good tablecloth, the one cross-stitched with blue birds and wild roses. Then minutes before supper, the fridge had arrived, delivered on the back of Mel Guthrie's pick-up truck.

This meant the kitchen floor had to be re-mopped, supper had to be re-heated, and with the ladies starting to arrive for the Prayer Meeting, there was no time left in which to admire the fridge.

'This hocus-pocus is starting to give me the creeps,' my

mother whispered. 'If it doesn't start to work pretty soon, I'm quitting. All that handshaking! All that smiling!' She raised her eyes mockingly upwards, and pulled her mouth into an abrupt meek smile.

I was tired of the Prayer Meetings too, but the longer I stayed in, the harder it seemed to get out. Miss Pym and Miss Pym caught my eye whenever possible, smiled at me, called me 'Our Young People'. Only last Thursday at Mrs Jack Hinkey's, they took me aside, held me by the wrist, and told me they were praying for me to join them in their mission field next summer.

I tried not to think about it.

I stepped over to the newly delivered refrigerator and opened its door to look at the automatic light, the built-in blue eggcups, the little swinging door that said 'Butter'. I had no concrete plans to mention the fridge, though the fridge was certainly worthy of mention. Its very presence gave the kitchen a bright and hopeful look.

From the next room, came various subdued creakings and rustlings, as well as the squeaking sounds of Miss Pym putting on her accordion.

My mother wiped the back of her neck with a dish towel, then snapped off the kitchen lights. 'Here goes,' she said, and walked into the front room to join the ladies.

The light of the open refrigerator was golden now, in the darkness of the kitchen.

What a good fridge this is, I thought, still looking into it. It's so big and white, so solid and definite. Every part fits. It didn't seem that anything very bad could happen to us with a fridge like this in the corner of our kitchen.

Standing there, I was at first only slightly aware of the sound of singing from the direction of the iced-over kitchen window.

That sounds exactly like a choir of angels, I thought. If I were to hear angels, right this minute, they would sound exactly like that.

I found, though, that when I paid attention, the sound did not change or go away. The sound wasn't my imagination, and it wasn't something like a loud car radio that simply passed on the road. It really did seem to be – incredibly – a choir of angels, and they were singing right outside the kitchen window. Their voices were muffled by the storm window, but all the same, they were real, forceful, unmistakable.

Sometimes the angels hummed, other times they sang, sometimes only one or two of them, sometimes all of them together. Sometimes their voices became higher and louder, and at other times they became lower and quieter. At one point they became so low and quiet that, standing there, my skin hot and prickling, I decided they must have at last gone away. But after only a moment, they rebounded in full force, singing together in perfect unison. Even through the double frosty windows, their voices were sure and faultless, almost it seemed, taunting.

I pushed the fridge door shut and hurried into the front room. I took my place on a vinyl-covered kitchen chair next to the accordioned Miss Pym. I was dazzled for a moment by the brightness of the lightbulb on the ceiling.

'Angels,' I said aloud. I found my voice was trembling. 'There's angels singing. In the yard. A bunch of them.'

I saw that the ladies were watching me in an odd, embarrassed way, as if I'd mentioned women's periods, pregnancy, or something worse. My mother's eyes were black in her round white face.

'Angels?' Olga Olanski said. 'Praise Jesus!'

'Yes,' Miss Pym and Miss Pym murmured, not quite together. 'Praise Jesus.'

My mother looked sideways toward the darkened kitchen, braced her hands against her knees and stood. She walked cautiously into the dark kitchen and switched on the lights. Olga Olanski followed her, the other ladies, and finally, myself. The fluorescent lights flickered several times, then caught.

My mother stood with her back to us, facing the window, listening. Then without a word, she dropped heavily to her knees on the green linoleum floor. She bent forward, stretching her arm alongside the refrigerator and unplugged it.

'Is it gone?' she asked me, a little out of breath, the black plug still in her hand.

It took me a minute to understand what was being asked of me. I sniffed, wiped my nose on the sleeve of my blouse, bent my head down and listened.

Outside, a truck passed on the road, rattling the dishes in the cupboards. Then there was nothing. Only the furnace, and the ticking of Amel's alarm clock from his bedroom off the kitchen.

'Don't harden your heart to Jesus,' the two tall thin ladies said to me later when they came to ask me to return to Prayer Meetings. 'Don't turn your back to the Lord.'

They sat on either side of me at the kitchen table, each one reaching for my hands with their thin cold ones.

'I have homework,' I said, pulling my hands back from theirs.

I stood without looking at them, but what I said was true. Career Day was coming at school and you had to have good marks to take part. I'd already signed up for Airline Stewardess, School Teacher, and Beauty Technician.

* * *

Amel was now finished his second piece of lemon meringue pie, and pushed himself back from the table. He reached above his head and stretched.

'That part about the moon and the tides was in that green book in Mrs Holland's room, remember?' I asked. I remembered clearly the black and white diagram with the curve of the earth and the moon, the tidy black arrows arcing between. I remembered the fingerprint of chocolate or blood on the upper right-hand corner of the page. 'No, wait, I remember it now,' I said, holding my fork in the air. 'The orange and the flashlight!'

'No, that's different,' Amel said, rubbing the back of his neck. 'I don't know. It don't make no sense. If the moon had that kind of effect on the earth, you would notice it. Not on the rivers maybe, but why don't you see it on the lakes?'

My dad straightened the peak of his cap. 'See?' he said. He looked at me, then my mother. His eyes were small points of blue. 'See? I don't go to school and I'm smarter than her.'

'It's probably the kind of thing,' Amel said, 'where they cook up some fancy theory because it sounds good. Take your watch. You go around telling everyone how expensive it is, diamonds and all, and pretty soon you got yourself convinced.'

Something hummed lightly, then stopped.

'But these diamonds *are* real,' I said, holding my wrist up as if to prove it.

'Sez who.'

My mother lifted a cup of tea to her lips and her goitre glugged, the sound of a drain opening. Quickly, she put her hand over it.

'Mrs Art Swanson's sister in North Battleford writes to some woman in the States,' my mother said, speaking quickly, 'You send money and somehow she cures you through the mail.'

Amel rubbed one side of his face with his hand, then reached up to check the sides of his hair.

'Her goitre started out the size of a potato, and is down to the size of a plum.' My mother looked at us, then started to cry, bending over the supper table and hanging onto the edge of it. 'I don't know which way to turn anymore.'

I unrolled the rollers at the front and sides of my hair, then folded my arms to hide my watch.

Amel reached for his parka which he'd left on the back of his chair.

'Well,' he said.

We felt the shock of the outside air as he left through the

kitchen door. In the room there was the smell of snow and motor oil.

The only sounds were the light musical hum of the fridge, and the relentless sound of my mother's weeping.

'Go back to the doctor,' I said. 'Try the other one. He might know something.'

'What good did the doctor do last time?' my dad said.

I pushed my chair back, then stood to clatter up the forks and spoons.

'You tell her what to do then,' I said. 'If you know, then tell her.'

I turned to the sink and opened the tap so quickly the water hammered in the pipes, vibrating the tap for a moment.

I thought of what the two tall thin ladies had said, that my heart had hardened. I pictured it, the size of my closed fist, hard, beautiful, reliable, made of gold and – yes – of diamonds.

From the faucet I took a stiff grey rag, a sleeve of my dad's or Amel's old underwear, and dropped it into the water.

What I wish is this, I thought, wringing out the dishrag. I held my breath, twisted the rag into a rope in my hands, and wished in a single wordless rush.

I wish to be like the angels outside the kitchen window / I wish to sing and hover and shine / I wish to be bright / I wish to be fearless / I wish to be amazing.

Paper Houses

I WAS SITTING with Woody on the couch in Morris and Regina's livingroom.

'Holy smokes,' Morris said, moving my purse under the coffee table to make room for his feet. 'What the heck do you keep in there, Irene? Pool balls?'

My purse was an ordinary imitation-leather handbag with a snap-up top, orange in colour, and I was always surprised – surprised and mildly alarmed – when people commented on it.

'Irene's got everything in there except a tire-jack,' Woody teased, his arm brushing lightly against mine. 'Isn't that so, Irene?'

'Make-up,' I said, used to jokes about my purse, 'a comb, let's see ... two apples, one boiled egg, spare nylons, a fold-up rain cap, money.' I didn't mention how much money. And I didn't mention the letter from Teachers' College either, the letter that began, 'We are pleased to advise your acceptance into Teachers' Training.' It was a letter I hadn't shown to anyone, not even Woody.

'Oh, money,' Morris said. 'That explains it.'

'It's gotta be the money,' Woody agreed.

Regina brought in a tray of coffee mugs. She was big-boned, blond, healthy-looking, and she was wearing plaid pants and a yellow top.

'White, white, black, the works,' she said, passing out the mugs. Then she sat down with a little puff.

'Cheers,' Morris said, and Woody held his coffee up to toast back.

I straightened Woody's ring on my hand, and he stretched his arm out behind me on the back of the couch. The ring was his RCMP Training Academy ring, which I wore with adhesive tape wound around the back of the band so it fit the ring finger of my left hand. The ring was a seriously-going-steady ring, a pre-engagement ring.

'At the telephone office,' I said, trying to be sociable, 'the other operators say that with a purse like mine under the switchboard, we don't have to worry about a hold-up. They say all we need to do is throw my purse and it would squash the robber like a fly.'

Woody and Morris had gone through RCMP training together, and were now two of the three Mounties posted to this town. Hold-ups were their department. I could see Morris run my strategy through his mind like film through a projector.

'It just might work,' he said, after a minute.

'It sure is worth a try, Irene,' Woody smiled.

'We bought that clock on our honeymoon,' Regina said, seeing me looking at a clock on the wall. The clock had a leather face with various pictures worked in leather around the circumference – a Mountie, a grizzly, a maple leaf, a snow-capped mountain.

'We were in Jasper,' Regina said, bending over to accommodate a brown-haired girl who was climbing onto her lap.

'Everywhere there's these goddamn ...' Morris stuck his fingers up beside his ears.

'Elk,' Regina said.

'Elk. First morning, there's these goddamn elk walking down the middle of the street. I swear I thought I was hung over.'

'That's because you were,' Regina said, and we laughed.

I rotated my left shoulder, then my right. I'd never had a serious boyfriend before, and was not used to the amount of work involved. Most nights, I was out with Woody until after midnight, then had to set my alarm for six to wash my hair, iron my clothes, and boil my eggs, the only food I had time to prepare. Sometimes, I thought I wouldn't have minded a week-end off, to lie in bed and read magazines.

'Regina,' said Woody, moving to the edge of the couch and bobbing his head and shoulders in a playful way, 'is that your smelly old mutt, Skippy, there on your lap?' He reached forward to tickle the little girl and she laughed.

'Listen to Skippy bark,' Woody said, tickling her again. 'Arf, arf. Listen.'

'It's Pammy!' the girl shrieked. 'It's me! It's Pammy!'

Morris stood up, accidentally scuffing against my purse again. 'Come on downstairs, Woody,' he said. 'You got to see the panelling I'm putting up.' As they went down, I heard him explain, 'There were two choices, dark or light.'

* * *

All the lights were off when Woody drove me home the night before. I crept in, trying to stay near the walls where the floor was less likely to creak, but it creaked anyway. 'There were some drunks yelling,' my mother's voice informed me from the pitch black of the front room.

Now that my dad stayed with his girlfriend Annie Karachuk, my mother slept on the couch to guard the house. She slept lightly, with her nylons rolled down to mid-calf, and her green corduroy bathrobe buttoned up and ready to go. The green bathrobe looked enough like a coat that she could run straight out into the yard and chase away drunks who broke bottles on the sidewalk or threw up into her cucumbers.

'It was from about eleven to twelve,' her voice said from the direction of the couch. She laid the information before me, the way a cat drops a mouse.

I leaned my cheek against the cool, smooth wall. My body ached with tiredness and the edgy, pulled-out-of-shape feeling I had after necking with Woody. What I wanted was to go to bed.

'They threw some kind of *viciousdart*,' she said, her words a blur.

I felt along the wall until I found the light switch, then

snapped it on. The overhead light hurt my eyes. I could smell
Woody's aftershave on my skin and hair.

'A what?'

'A viciousdart.' She reached for the object from the window
ledge and held it out to me. It was a grey metal lawn dart with
a red plastic feather.

Then I understood, *vicious dart*. When my mother was
woken by drunks and trespassers, she stayed up for a while and
studied the *It Pays to Enrich Your Word Power* section from the
pile of Reader's Digests she had stacked beside the couch.

I had a pile of them in my own bedroom for the same fea-
ture. The answers were often underlined in both our pencils.
This was a coincidence I didn't care to examine too closely.

'It's for a game,' I said. 'Like horseshoes.'

'I phoned the RCMP and he said I could come in and file a
report. He didn't give a hoot.'

I was completely awake now. I tried to recall who would
have been on duty, and guessed it was Morris.

'Not like that other one,' she continued. 'I got the other
one last time and he was so nice. He said, ''You shouldn't have
to put up with that.'' He really seemed to care.'

She started to cry, remembering his kindness. This was
another thing we had in common. If someone was too nice to
me, I couldn't take it either.

'I'm old and good for nothing,' she said, crying. 'Why am I
living? Why shouldn't drunks throw darts at me? What else am
I good for?'

I knew it would insult her if I looked at my watch.

'I'm old. I've got nothing to live for.'

* * *

'That's our *Universal Book of Knowledge*,' Regina said, indicat-
ing a row of green books underneath the TV. 'Go ahead and
look at one. Please feel free.' She pulled out a volume from
one end and handed it to me.

I sat down on the couch and cracked the book open to a cross-section of an igloo with an Eskimo family inside.

'We were specially selected,' Regina offered, pink-cheeked. She hesitated, then went on. 'The salesman interviewed us and we scored over a hundred. He gave us a special rate. So long as we promised to show it to friends and neighbours.' She turned to check on the books that sat in a perfect line on the shelf.

'Do you want to see the picture?' I asked Pammy. Her face was level with my own. 'I'll show you a house made out of snow.'

Pammy put her hand out to hold on to her mother's plaid pantleg.

She wasn't a terribly nice-looking child, I noticed. With her wide-spaced eyes, her tiny nose, and her wide mouth, she looked a bit like a turtle.

Regina knelt to push Pammy's bangs back with her hand. 'Look at her baby hair,' she said to me, and moved the girl to the window so I could have a better look.

There was fine downy hair along the girl's hairline. Pammy tried to squirm away, but Regina held on to her for a moment longer.

'See it?' Regina asked. 'I'm going to cry myself to sleep the day that baby hair falls out.'

There was the sound of yelling and running on the basement stairs, then Woody and Morris burst into the kitchen.

'Pammy!' Morris called. 'Skippy can play volleyball!' And he tapped a red balloon up into the air. When it started to come down, the black dog jumped at it, its teeth snapping, bouncing the balloon up again. Woody tapped it up from the other side of the kitchen, and the dog snapped it up again.

The lights were still off inside, but the balloon caught the light from the late afternoon sun. The red balloon, filled with light, bounced lightly one way, then the other, while the black dog jumped and jumped at it. Then someone missed, and the dog cornered the balloon on the floor.

'Look out!' Regina shrieked, and covered Pammy's ears with her hands. The balloon popped and everyone laughed.

'Come on, Pammy,' said Woody. 'You try it.'

'Downstairs!' said Regina, pointing.

When Morris and Woody went down with Pammy and Skippy, Regina snapped on the kitchen light. 'That old mutt's more fun than a wind-up monkey,' she laughed.

* * *

At the telephone office, I wore earphones, and sat on a stool beside four other operators. Before me was a section of the switchboard, and a row of switches. When a number on the switchboard clicked, I plugged it in, then connected them with the number they wanted.

At first, I listened in to people's conversations when I got the chance, but I was surprised how little most people said on the phone. Most people talked about their health, or the prices of things. Some people just said, 'Number five drill bit by two o'clock,' not even hello or good-bye.

Even Annie Karachuk, my father's girlfriend, talked mostly about the cross-stitch embroideries she did and sold around town. 'I'll make those petals that nice pale pink, number two, and get darker toward the tips, number six, then maybe number nine. But more colours is going to cost you extra.'

Sometimes I didn't answer Annie Karachuk's number at all. Sometimes I just sat and watched it buzz and flap like a fly stuck to a strip of flypaper. She was in my section of the board, so if she wanted to make a call, Monday to Friday, eight to five, she had to get past me.

If the supervisor was in, I had to answer.

'Number please,' I said once, in the crisp nasal sing-song I'd picked up from the other operators.

'It was never my intention to hurt you, Irene,' Annie Karachuk's voice said right away. 'I want you to know that.'

Intention. What an odd, formal word for her to use, I

thought. I wondered if Annie Karachuk was enriching her word power also.

I noticed too, that she spoke the words in a flat, halting way, as if she'd written down what she wanted to say on the back of an embroidery order, then read it aloud over the phone.

I listened though. Then I couldn't think of anything to say.

'That's all right,' I said finally.

'That's quite all right,' is what I later told Woody I said. In my head, I said it in an English accent. Most of the answers I composed to Annie Karachuk in my head afterwards required an English accent.

Oh, my dear, think nothing of it.

You simply must not trouble yourself on my behalf.

Intentions, yes. Intentions, how interesting.

Later, when Woody and I were driving around, I couldn't stop talking about Annie Karachuk. I turned to Woody.

'Arrest her,' I said.

'I can't just arrest her out of the blue,' Woody said. 'She didn't do anything wrong.'

I just stared at the yellow headlights on the road ahead.

'Maybe what she did wasn't right,' Woody said, taking his hands off the wheel and holding his flattened palms up in the air for a second. 'I'm not saying for a minute that it was. But if we're talking about the Criminal Code of Canada, I have to tell you, Irene, what she did wasn't against the law.'

We were near the lights of her house now. She lived just a few miles out of town, in the middle of a grassy field.

'Let's drive around her house,' I said. I was turning his ring around on my finger. 'I want to see the other side.'

'I don't want to lose my job, Irene,' Woody said, but he steered the off-duty patrol car across the ditch and through the grass. He turned out the headlights and we circled silently, no sound but the grass rubbing on the underside of the car.

I saw a chair with a tasselled cushion on it. I saw a gilt-framed picture of the Last Supper.

Just behind Annie Karachuk's flowery kitchen curtains, I saw my father's hand. His hand was perfectly still, and he was holding a piece of toast.

* * *

Another morning when I was walking to work, I saw my father on the sidewalk. He didn't have to go to work that early, and I saw he hadn't shaved yet, but I refused to ask him where he was going.

He reached into his pocket for his roll of money when he saw me, and started peeling bills off, one by one.

I watched, but didn't stop him. I knew he must hate it, and felt the quickest flash of pity for him, peeling off the bills like so much Monopoly money, feeling the corner of each one to make sure there weren't two stuck together.

Finally, I must have moved or blinked, because he stopped, and held the money out to me.

'I don't want your money,' I said, but took it right away, in case he changed his mind.

'When a man is in the bush,' my father said, looking up and down the road as if he'd lost something, but had no real hope of getting it back, 'when a man is in the bush, he goes one way and the bush looks that way. Then when he tries to go back, everything looks different.'

I noticed he had deeper hollows in his cheeks now. Annie Karachuk's cooking must not be so great, I thought.

'If a man thinks too much, he's going to get lost. He just got to do what looks like it's right,' he said. He looked at me, his pale blue eyes watery as they often were in the morning.

I held the money rolled so tight in my hand, Woody's ring cut into my finger.

'There's too much blackflies in the bush for me,' I said.

'I find the insect population highly inconducive to a stroll in the woods,' is what I later told Woody I said.

In the washroom at the telephone office, I counted my

money. My dad'd given me seven hundred and twenty-four dollars. I sorted the bills by denomination, rolled an elastic around them, and put them in my purse along with my letter from Teachers' College.

* * *

I sat at the kitchen table and peeled carrots for Regina. Downstairs, there was thumping and laughing, then the bang of a balloon. The skin of the carrot fell onto the table in loopy strips, like orange ribbon.

When I looked up, it seemed to me that everything looked very lovely, perfect, fragile. It looked like the whole house was made of paper.

Maybe it was paper, I thought. Maybe this was all a trick, like *Candid Camera*. Maybe Regina, Morris and Pammy were playing rehearsed parts, maybe Skippy was some stray from the pound.

I was pretty sure this was a crazy notion, but kept my eyes open anyway, looking at the pale yellow walls, the blue pots, the alphabet magnets on the fridge, to see if they were real. The harder I looked, the more it seemed to me that everything might be made of paste and paper. Everything looked a little too perfect, the way models of things can look more perfect than the things they represent.

I got up and walked around. I went into the living room then further along the shag-carpeted hall to the bathroom, where I stared at lipsticks and potty chairs and shampoo bottles. I looked across the hall at the chenille bedspread in Regina and Morris's bedroom, and at the plastic blow-up letters arranged across the head of the bed, a pink L, blue O, yellow V, green E, L O V E.

It seemed to me that if I looked at things from a certain angle, I might be able to see how it'd been done, that I might discover the trick behind it. Maybe, I told myself, at a certain angle, the illusion would break down, and everything would disappear.

Then I heard Pammy and the men pounding up the stairs to

supper. I stepped back into the bathroom, flushed the toilet, then went back to the kitchen.

We sat down around the supper Regina had laid out – pink salmon loaf, fluffy mounds of mashed potatoes, carrots shiny with butter, cloverleaf rolls.

Pammy refused to sit in her highchair and sat instead on a regular chair bolstered by three volumes of the *Universal Book of Knowledge*.

I served myself large portions and ate quickly.

'More salmon loaf?' Regina asked. 'More rolls?'

'Yes, please,' I said. 'Thank you.'

Finally, Regina got up and set cereal bowls of a creamy fruit mixture before us. There was no sound except the scraping of spoons, and the ticking of the clock from the living room.

'Regina, Regina,' Morris said. 'You cook like an angel.'

Regina smiled at him, then turned to me, her cheeks flushed pink.

'It's called ambrosia. You take one can of mandarins, one can of pineapple, add whipped cream, shredded coconut, and baby marshmallows. It takes no more than five minutes.'

Woody pressed his hand on my leg and held it there a minute. Then he moved his chair back from the table and stretched.

'You've topped yourself, Regina,' he said. 'You've gone and set a new record.' He took my hand, and stood.

'You driving that car that misses second?' Morris asked, and the men went out.

'Everything looks pretty good with you and Woody,' Regina said. She was wiping Pammy's face with a wet cloth, making a game of it, wiping her arm, then her left cheek, her ankle, then her right cheek.

'Oh, sure,' I answered.

'He never brought a girl for supper before.'

From the front of the house, the car honked.

I got my heavy purse from where I'd left it in the

livingroom, opened it and searched through it quickly, until I found the letter from Teachers' College. I unfolded it and smoothed it flat on a clean spot on the table in front of Regina.

'I got this letter,' I told her.

Pammy got off Regina's knee and started tugging at her hand.

Regina looked down at the letter, then with Pammy still tugging at her, looked up at me.

'They spelled my name wrong,' I said.

'Teachers' College?' Regina said. 'That's what you're going to do?'

'Sometimes, I think I'd like to be a teacher,' I said, trying to talk above the sound of Pammy crying. 'But I think the feeling tends to disappear when I'm around children.'

'Does Woody know?' Regina asked, jiggling Pammy on her hip.

'Not yet.'

Outside, the car honked again and I took the letter back, folded it and put it in my orange purse.

'Well, I'd better go.'

'Come say goodbye to Irene,' Regina said, putting Pammy down and leading her to the door. 'Say thank you for coming, Irene.'

Pammy looked up at me and leaned toward her mother. 'Stupid,' she said. 'Stupid Irene.'

'No,' Regina said, her neck blotchy. 'We don't say stupid. Stupid's not a nice word.' She knelt and touched the tip of her finger to the girl's cheek. 'Say silly. Irene is a silly girl. Silly's all right.'

'Anyway,' I said, 'thank you for supper. It was delicious.'

'Please come again,' Regina said.

It was cold outside, but my face and hands felt scorched, as if I'd been standing around an open fire. From the steps, I could see the men holding a flashlight and laughing into the hood of the car.

I made my way down the dark steps. Near the bottom, I stepped on something with wheels, a child's car, or possibly a roller skate. Instantly, I shot forward, dropped a level, skated crazily down a section of driveway, flew off, then somehow, in the darkness, landed on my feet.

It felt lucky. It felt right. It felt like the omen I was looking for.

I stood very still and looked at the yellow windows of the house. Then I walked to the road.

Blessing

'YOU NEED TO get a phone,' I told my mother when she opened her door.

'Why do I need to get a phone?' she answered. 'So more salesmen can pester me? I already bought my cemetery plot. It's not like I'm going to need another one.'

She was wearing a flowery blouse with rhinestone buttons, the rhinestone on the middle one missing, and baggy pants, purple and criss-crossed with silver threads – evening wear originally, but patched now with squares of denim on both knees.

'Where's Norman?' she asked, shielding her eyes against the sun with one hand. 'Did Norman come?'

Maybe it wasn't exactly an accent she had. Maybe it was an attitude, an Old Country way of looking at things. In any case, the way she said, 'Norman' – with combined emphasis and deference – gave the name a foreign, almost noble sound. Two scrawny white cats arched themselves against my legs, tested their claws against my Indian print skirt.

'Norman couldn't come,' I told her. I was hanging onto my overnight bag and trying to scoop the cats away with my foot. 'Norman had to work.'

I leaned over to unhook the cats' claws from my skirt then followed Mother up the steep porch steps, past cardboard boxes of jars and what looked like old clothes. I'd had to get up at five for Norman to drive me to the bus depot, I'd been on the bus till noon, a nun in a brown habit had sloshed Orange Crush on my foot, and besides all that, I'd used up a day of holiday leave.

It was cooler inside the house and the kitchen had its same sour, salty smell. The cupboards were still red and blue, each door bordered with pictures of flowers cut from seed catalogues, glued on, then covered with clear nail polish. The window was crowded with African violets, geraniums, and various cuttings rooting in jars. Under the window sill and along the counter were stacks of margarine containers, jars of keys, tacks, ballpoints.

If I turn around, I thought, I'll knock something.

'Why don't you write?' I said. 'I never hear from you. I got worried. I thought maybe something happened to you.'

'Oh! Me ...' She waved her hand as if swishing away a fly. 'I'm old and good for nothing. What difference does it make if something happens to me?'

She stooped into the cupboard and brought out a tin of cookies I recognized as part of a parcel I sent at Christmas. She took the lid off the cookies, placed them in the centre of the table and sighed.

'It's not,' she said, 'like I have something to live for. It's not like I have grandchildren.'

'I'll get this bag out of the way,' I told her with the same brisk cheer I used to deal with stubborn customers at the bank. I took my overnight bag to the front room where a couch faced a large TV.

There were family and religious pictures everywhere – on the wall, on a bureau, on the TV. Red and white tissue paper dahlias decorated the pictures on the wall.

The top of the TV was arranged like an altar. On an embroidered runner were more tissue paper flowers in a vase, and pictures of Baby. One shadowy photo, taken from a larger photograph and then enlarged, showed her clinging to the hem of someone's skirt. Another picture, taken at the Stampede, showed her wearing a cowboy hat.

I could see how Baby's hand flared out where her thumb met her wrist. How could have I forgotten this – the squarish shape of her hand?

In the kitchen, my mother was pouring raspberry wine into

glasses. As a way of using up her extra berries, she always made her own.

Her purple and silver pants didn't bother me as they once would have. Thrift had become fashionable, and anyway, I told myself, maybe it was time to come to terms with these things.

'How's your arthritis?' I asked her. 'It doesn't look like your arthritis is any worse.'

The wine was sweet, like sherry, and the cookies, which I softened by dipping into the wine, were surprisingly tasty too.

'On TV, they said that royal jelly would do some good,' she said. 'Fifteen dollars a bottle. But I didn't see a difference.'

I told her about the new manager at the bank and the comb lines in his hair. I told her about Norman's recent promotion, making more than I meant to make of it. I told her about a party, where we were supposed to go dressed as our favourite movie characters.

'Cathy Myzychin had twins again,' Mother said, looking up at me, then down to her glass of wine on the table. 'Blue eyes and blond hair, both of them like Danny.'

'Danny changing diapers?' I poured myself another tall glass of scarlet wine. 'We always thought Danny would end up in Hollywood. Either that or jail, remember?'

'They're family people,' Mother continued stubbornly. 'Not the type to gad around. Or fritter their money. They know what counts. Cathy drives them to the store and leaves them in the van to get groceries. It won't hurt them to cry, I told her. It prepares them for life.' She screwed the top back on the wine and replaced it in the cupboard. 'Now they have five. The oldest starts school in the fall.'

'Five?' I asked, slurping down another soggy cookie.

'Without children,' she said, 'you have nothing.'

* * *

'You've had these cats for ages,' I said, still cheerful from the raspberry wine. The cat's fur burned against my hand from the heat of the sun.

The two cats slept on an inverted metal washtub beside the house. On the ground there was a dish cut from the bottom of a plastic vinegar bottle, and in the dish, a crust of bread that looked like it'd been soaked in milk.

'You have to feed them cat food,' I told my mother. 'Cats can't live on bread and milk.'

'Mine can,' she countered. 'They like it. They eat porridge too.' She was sliding her feet into old cracked dress shoes she wore to work in the garden.

I picked up one of the bony cats and it submitted for a moment, then freed itself.

'They're females from the same batch,' Mother said, and got the hoe from the porch. 'They disappear sometimes, but they're back when they're good and hungry.' She was hoeing now, walking backwards, loosening the grey soil between the staked peas. 'The modern type. Right in style.'

'In style?'

'They gallivant around town, no kittens, at least not here. I guess they need the freedom to find themselves.' Her tanned faced crinkled into a smile as if she'd said something hilarious.

An insect on the poplar in the next yard buzzed like an electric wire.

'Why shouldn't they gallivant around?' I said. 'Since when is that a crime?'

Why shouldn't they have the freedom to find themselves, I'd almost said. Where had my mother got that expression, 'the freedom to find themselves'? She must have heard it on TV. Surely, I'd never said anything that corny.

'You think gallivanting around town is so terrible,' I said, raising my voice to make sure she heard me. 'Well, maybe they don't. Maybe they like it.'

She kept on hoeing, as if she hadn't heard me.

I was standing on a board that marked a division in the

garden. The garden itself was a jigsaw of tubs and levels and plots, all ruthlessly ordered according to a plan understood by no one but herself. Only she knew where to step or not to step.

'Why is it always like this?' I called out to her. 'I wish I didn't bother to come.'

At the end of her row, she looked back at me.

'Child, child,' she said in Ukrainian, and one of her rhinestones flashed like fire.

Then she switched back to English. 'I always have to walk on eggs around you.'

* * *

At the store near my mother's I bought cat food, brown bread and sour cream. I'd found a row of spinach in Mother's garden and decided to make spinach soup.

Downtown had moved almost to our house. This store was huge and bright and had talking cash registers. A Kentucky Fried Chicken had sprung up on the highway where a patch of bush used to be.

This was the same patch of bush where Baby and I had once planted our garden. Our mother'd let us use a sliver of her own garden – the strip between her corn and the fence. But she said only peas or beans would grow there, she told us how deep to plant the seeds, and how far apart. Baby and I wanted our own garden where we could plant what we wanted.

Back in my mother's kitchen, I fried an onion in butter and took a bowl into the garden to pick spinach leaves. Mother, now hoeing cabbages, hurried over. Her grey broom of hair was starting to fall out of the white bandana she'd tied around it.

'I'll wash it,' she said, taking the spinach from me. She poured water into a little tub and rinsed the spinach leaves.

'I could have done that.' I'd almost forgotten. Vegetables were washed by the back door and the water used for the garden.

When the soup was ready, I called her.

'Oh,' she said when she tasted it, 'it's good.'

I couldn't believe how pleased I was. 'I made up the recipe myself,' I said. 'I got the idea when I saw your spinach.'

Mother dipped her bread into the soup and allowed her bowl to be refilled.

'When we left the Old Country, Mama's mother wouldn't say goodbye,' she said. She got up, turned on the flame under the kettle, then sat down again.

'Your great-grandmother,' she said. 'She wouldn't speak or give her blessing. That's what Mama wanted, for her to wish us well, but she was mad and wouldn't talk. Not even goodbye.

'The whole village came to the train station with us. Everyone walked down the road together, singing and crying. When we came to Baba's house, we all stopped in front. Mama sent me in to say goodbye.' She traced the pattern on the plastic lace tablecloth with her finger.

'What happened?'

'I went to the door,' my mother continued, 'but she wouldn't unlatch it. I was just tall enough to look in the open window. But she had her back to me. She was cleaning ashes out of the stove.

'I said, ''Baba, we're going''. But she kept on sweeping ashes.'

'How could she be like that?' I said.

'She could be any way she wanted.'

'That's terrible. That's so terrible.'

The kettle began to shriek, and Mother stood up to turn off the flame.

'It must have been awful,' I said, 'leaving like that.'

'What's done is done. No one can change it now.'

* * *

Baby's clothes lay folded in the bedroom drawers. I held up a little embroidered blouse, originally made from a sugar sack and trimmed with lace. The faint lettering of the sugar sack was still visible on the back, and the front was embroidered with blue birds and wild roses.

'Take it for your own daughter,' my mother said, appearing from behind me.

'Not now. If I decide to have a baby I might.'

I put the blouse back into the drawer and stood by the window, looking at the puffs of dust along the highway by the new Kentucky Fried Chicken.

I thought of the garden Baby and I had planted there, of how we'd grown five potatoes the size of marbles. My mother appeared beside me again.

'Here's a surprise for you,' she said, and passed a white wrapped bundle from her shoulder to mine.

There was something about the gesture, her left shoulder to mine, the care in the passing. Without hesitating, my hands reached for the blanket, but the instant I touched it, maybe before I touched it, I knew I'd been tricked.

The bundle was stiff, and light as a shoe-box. Smiling blankly up from the white blanket in my hands was a plaster doll's face. The doll had once been mine, and later, Baby's. The end of its nose was chipped, but its mouth still held a perfect rosebud smile.

Without speaking, I tossed the doll on the bed. There was a light click as the eyes shut and a soft ticking as the mechanism inside the doll's head swung back and forth. In front of the Kentucky Fried Chicken a group of people leaned against a car, talking. A large man with a cowboy hat said something to make them laugh.

I had a stupid part to my brain. I had a part that didn't understand, no matter how often I went over something. I didn't understand, for example, how that bush could be cut down just like that. How was it, that a thing could be so done and over with?

* * *

'Don't be mad,' my mother said on the way to the bus depot. 'I didn't mean to make you mad.'

The two cats were following us up the dark street. The sidewalk was lit at wide intervals, and moths batted themselves against the yellow lights.

I didn't answer. The dark air was warm as blood.

Mother carried my bag while I carried a heavy cardboard box tied with twine. The box contained two quart jars of dill pickles and two of beet. The twine cut into my fingers and at the corner I put the box down for a moment, almost on top of the two white cats who'd followed us.

'I have to go back or they'll get lost,' my mother said, and it took me a few seconds to understand she was talking about the cats.

The bus depot at the Princess Hotel was only another block away, and we could see from where we stood that the bus wasn't in yet.

'O K,' I said. 'Sure. Why not?' And I filed this in my head along with the other things I was saving to tell Norman. All of a sudden, these half-starved cats mattered more than seeing me to the bus.

'Maybe you won't want to come back,' she said.

I tried my bag on top of the box, then beside it. Then I looked up and saw her standing there, her back to the streetlight, watching me, her lips moving slightly, as if she was trying to make out fine print.

I leaned over, without expecting to – the gesture made easy by city ways – and kissed her. Her cheek was so soft and warm I was startled. She felt as small and fragile as a child. She smiled tightly, embarrassed. I hadn't kissed her since I was little.

'You better go,' she said. 'It's coming.'

Large white headlights approached steadily, far off from the dark road to the left.

I picked up the bag with one hand, the box by the twine with the other, and hurried across the road. I turned to see her, but could barely make her out, a small figure walking back along the sidewalk. A faint cobweb of light glimmered once off her silver-threaded pants.

'See you,' I called across the darkened street.

But with the bus approaching, I couldn't tell if she heard me.

I could still see the cats moving slowly back along the side-walk, grey smudges on the blackness. Then I couldn't see either the cats or my mother at all.

CANADIAN CATALOGUING IN PUBLICATION DATA

Borsky, Mary, 1946-
Influence of the moon

ISBN 0-88984-163-2

I. Title.

PS8553.07715 1995   C813'.54   C95-932341-4
PR9199.3.B6715 1995

Published by The Porcupine's Quill, Inc., 68 Main Street, Erin, Ontario NOB 1TO, with financial assistance from The Canada Council and the Ontario Arts Council. The support of the Government of Ontario through the Ministry of Culture, Tourism and Recreation is also gratefully acknowledged, as is the support of the Department of Canadian Heritage through the Book and Periodical Industry Development programme and the Periodical Distribution Assistance Programme.

Represented in Canada by the Literary Press Group. Trade orders are available from General Distribution Services.

Readied for the press by John Metcalf.
Copy edited by Doris Cowan.

Cover is after a collage by Tony Calzetta.